Strong and Steady / Or, Paddle Your Own Canoe

Horatio Alger Jr.

Table of Contents

PREFACE.

"Strong and Steady" is the third volume of the "Luck and Pluck Series." Though the story is quite distinct from its predecessors, it is intended to illustrate the same general principle. Walter Conrad, the hero, is unexpectedly reduced from affluence to poverty, and compelled to fight his own way in life. Undaunted by misfortune, he makes up his mind to "paddle his own canoe," and, declining the offers of friends, sets to work with a resolute will and persistent energy, which command success in the end.

Hoping that Walter's adventures may prove of interest to his young readers, and win the same favorable verdict which has been pronounced upon his previous books, the author takes his leave for the present, with many thanks for the generous welcome so often accorded to him.

October 15, 1871.

CHAPTER I. THE ESSEX CLASSICAL INSTITUTE.

"You've got a nice room here, Walter."

"Yes, you know I am to stay here two years, and I might as well be comfortable."

"It's ever so much better than my room—twice as big, to begin with. Then, my carpet looks as if it had come down through several generations. I'll bet the old lady had it when she was first married. As for a mirror, I've got a seven-by-nine looking-glass that I have to look into twice before I can see my whole face. As for the bedstead, it creaks so when I jump into it that I expect every night it'll fall to pieces like the 'one hoss shay,' and spill me on the floor. Now your room is splendidly furnished."

"Yes, it is now, but father furnished it at his own expense. He said he was willing to lay out a little money to make me comfortable."

"That's more than my father said. He told me it wouldn't do me any harm to rough it."

"I don't know but he is right," said Walter. "Of course I don't object to the new carpet and furniture,"—and he looked with pleasure at the handsome carpet with its bright tints, the black walnut bookcase with its glass doors, and the tasteful chamber furniture,—"but I shouldn't consider it any hardship if I had to rough it, as you call it."

"Wouldn't you? Then I'll tell you what we'll do. We'll change rooms. You can go round and board at Mrs. Glenn's, and I'll come here. What do you say?"

"I am not sure how my father would look on that arrangement," said Walter, smiling.

"I thought you'd find some way out," said Lemuel. "For my part, I don't believe you'd fancy roughing it any better than I."

"I don't know," said Walter; "I've sometimes thought I shouldn't be very sorry to be a poor boy, and have to work my own way."

"That's very well to say, considering you are the son of a rich man."

"So are you."

"Yes, but I don't get the benefit of it, and you do. What would you do now if you were a poor boy?"

"I can't say, of course, now, but I would go to work at something. I am sure I could earn my own living."

"I suppose I could, but I shouldn't want to."

"You're lazy, Lem, that's what's the matter with you."

"I know I am," said Lemuel, good-naturedly. "Some people are born lazy, don't you think so?"

"Perhaps you are right," answered Walter, with a smile. "Now suppose we open our Cæsar."

"I suppose we might as well. Here's another speech. I wish those old fellows hadn't been so fond of speech-making. I like the accounts of battles well enough, but the speeches are a bother."

"I like to puzzle them out, Lem."

"So don't I. How much have we got for a lesson?"

"Two sections."

While the boys are at work reading these two sections, two-thirds of the work being done by Walter, whose head is clearer and whose knowledge greater than his companion's, a little explanation shall be given, in order that we may better understand the position and prospects of the two boys introduced.

Of Lemuel Warner, it need only be said that he was a pleasant-looking boy of fourteen, the son of a prosperous merchant in New York. Walter Conrad was from a small inland town, where his father was the wealthiest and most prominent and influential citizen, having a handsome mansion-house, surrounded by extensive grounds.

How rich he was, was a matter of conjecture; but he was

generally rated as high as two hundred thousand dollars. Mrs. Conrad had been dead for five years, so that Walter, who was an only child, had no immediate relation except his father. It was for this reason, perhaps, that he had been sent to the Essex Classical Institute, of which we find him a member at the opening of our story. Being a boy of talent, and well grounded in Latin, he was easily able to take a high rank in his class. Lemuel Warner had become his intimate friend, being in the same class, but considerably inferior to him in scholarship. They usually got their Latin lessons together, and it was owing to this circumstance that Lemuel made a better figure in his recitations than before Walter became a member of the school.

"There, that job's done," said Lemuel, closing his book with an air of satisfaction. "Now we can rest."

"You forget the Latin exercise."

"Oh, bother the Latin exercise! I don't see what's the use of writing Latin any way. English composition is hard enough. What's to be done?"

"You know the doctor expects each boy to write a letter in Latin, addressed to his father, not less than twelve lines in length."

"It isn't to be sent home, is it? Mr. Warner senior, I reckon, would stare a little when he got his. He wouldn't know Latin from Cherokee."

"Possibly your Latin won't differ much from Cherokee, Lem."

"What's the use of being sarcastic on a fellow, and hurting his feelings?" said Lem, laughing in a way to show that his feelings were not very seriously hurt. "I say, couldn't one crib a little from Cæsar?"

"Not very well, considering the doctor is slightly familiar with that author."

"I wonder whether Cæsar used to write home to his father when he was at boarding-school. If he did, I should like to get hold of some of his letters."

"They would probably have to be altered considerably to adapt them to the present time."

"Well, give me a sheet of paper and I'll begin."

The boys undertook their new task, and finished it by nine o'clock. I should be glad to furnish a copy of Lemuel's letter, which was written with brilliant disregard of grammatical rules; but unfortunately the original, afterwards considerably revised in accordance with suggestions from Walter, has not been preserved.

"I've a great mind to send my letter home, Walter," said Lemuel. "Father expects me to write home every week, and this would save me some trouble. Besides, he'd think I was getting on famously, to write home in Latin."

"Yes, if he didn't find out the mistakes."

"That's the rub. He'd show it to the minister the first time he called, and then my blunders would be detected. I guess I'd better wait till it comes back from the doctor corrected."

"I expect to hear from home to-morrow," said Walter.

"Why to-morrow in particular? Do you generally get letters Thursday?"

"No, my letters generally come on Saturday, and I answer them Sunday. But to-morrow is my birthday."

"Is it? Let me be the first to congratulate you. How venerable will you be?"

"As venerable as most boys of fifteen, Lem."

"You're three months older than I am, then. Do you expect a present?"

"I haven't thought much about it, but I don't believe father will forget me."

"Can't you guess what you are likely to get?"

"I can guess, but I may not be right. Father promised to give me a gold watch-chain some time. You know I have a gold watch already."

"Yes, and a regular little beauty."

"So it wouldn't surprise me much to get a chain for a present."

"You're a lucky boy. My watch is silver, and only cost twenty dollars."

"I dare say I should be just as happy with a silver watch, Lem."

"I suppose you wouldn't like to buy, would you? If so, I'll give you the chance. A fair exchange is no robbery."

"No, I suppose not; but it wouldn't do to exchange a gift."

"Perhaps, if my watch were gold and yours silver, you wouldn't have any objections."

"I don't think that would alter the case with me. A gift is a gift, whether it is more or less valuable."

"How long have you had your watch, Walter?"

"Ever since my thirteenth birthday."

"I have had mine a year. I broke the crystal and one of the hands the very first day."

"That was pretty hard usage, Lem."

"The watch had a pretty good constitution, so it has survived to the present day. But I'm getting sleepy, Walter. It's the hard study, I suppose, that's done it. I must be getting back to Ma'am Glenn's. Good-night."

"Good-night, Lem."

Lemuel Warner gathered up his books, and left the room. Walter poked the fire, putting some ashes on, so that it would keep till the next morning, and commenced undressing. He had scarcely commenced, however, when a heavy step was heard on the stairs, and directly afterwards a knock resounded upon his door.

Wondering who his late visitor could be, Walter stepped

to the door, and opened it.

CHAPTER II. IN THE CARS.

If Walter was surprised at receiving a visit at so late an hour, he was still more surprised to recognize in the visitor Dr. Porter, the principal of the Institute.

"Good-evening, Conrad," said the doctor. "I am rather a late visitor. I was not sure but you might be in bed."

"I was just getting ready to go to bed, sir. Won't you walk in?"

"I will come in for five minutes only."

"Take the rocking-chair, sir."

All the while Walter was wondering what could be the doctor's object in calling. He was not conscious of having violated any of the regulations of the Institute, and even had he done so, it would be unusual for the principal to call upon him at such an hour. So he watched the doctor with a puzzled glance, and waited to hear him state his errand.

"Have you heard from home lately, Conrad?" asked the doctor.

"Yes, sir, I received a letter a few days since."

"Did your father speak of being unwell?"

"No, sir," said Walter, taking instant alarm. "Have—have you heard anything?"

"Yes, my boy; and that is my reason for calling upon you at this unusual hour. I received this telegram twenty minutes since."

Walter took the telegram, with trembling fingers, and read the following message:—

"Dr. Porter:—Please send Walter Conrad home by the first train. His father is very sick.

"Nancy Forbes."

"Do you think there is any danger, Dr. Porter?" asked Walter, with a pale face.

"I cannot tell, my boy; this telegram furnishes all the information I possess. Who is Nancy Forbes?"

"She is the house-keeper. I can't realize that father is so sick. He did not say anything about it when he wrote."

"Let us hope it is only a brief sickness. I think you had better go home by the first train to-morrow morning."

"Yes, sir."

"I believe it starts at half-past seven."

"I shall be ready, sir."

"By the way, are you provided with sufficient money to pay your railway fare? If not, I will advance you the necessary sum."

"Thank you, sir, I have five dollars by me, and that will be more than sufficient."

"Then I believe I need not stay any longer," and the doctor rose.

"Don't think too much of your father's sickness, but try to get a good night's sleep. I hope we shall soon have you coming back with good news."

The principal shook hands with Walter and withdrew.

When his tall form had vanished, Walter sat down and tried to realize the fact of his father's sickness; but this he found difficult.

Mr. Conrad had never been sick within his remembrance, and the thought that he might become so had never occurred to Walter. Besides, the telegram spoke of him as *very* sick. Could there be danger?

That was a point which he could not decide, and all that remained was to go to bed. It was a long time before he got to sleep, but at length he did sleep, waking in time only for a hasty preparation for the homeward journey. He was so occupied with thoughts of his father that it was not till the journey was half finished, that it occurred to him that this was his fifteenth birthday, to which he had been looking forward for some time.

The seat in front of our hero was for some time vacant;

but at the Woodville station two gentlemen got in who commenced an animated conversation. Walter did not at first pay any attention to it. He was looking out of the window listlessly, unable to fix his mind upon anything except his father's sickness. But at length his attention was caught by some remarks, made by one of the gentlemen in front, and from this point he listened languidly.

"I suspected him to be a swindler when he first came to me," said the gentleman sitting next the window. "He hadn't an honest look, and I was determined not to have anything to do with his scheme."

"He was very plausible."

"Yes, he made everything look right on paper. That is easy enough. But mining companies are risky things always. I once got taken in to the tune of five thousand dollars, but it taught me a lesson. So I was not particularly impressed with the brilliant prospectus of the Great Metropolitan Mining Company, in spite of its high-sounding name, and its promised dividend of thirty per cent. Depend upon it, James Wall and his confederates will pocket all the dividends that are made."

"Very likely you are right. But it may be that Wall really believed there is a good chance of making money."

"Of course he did, but he was determined to make the money for himself, and not for the stockholders."

"I might have been tempted to invest, but all my money was locked up at the time, and I could not have done so without borrowing the money, and that I was resolved not to do."

"It was fortunate for you that you didn't, for the bubble has already burst."

"Is it possible? I was not aware of that."

"I thought you knew it. The news is in this morning's paper. There will be many losers. By the way, I hear that Mr. Conrad, of Willoughby, was largely interested."

"Then, of course, he is a heavy loser. Can he stand it?"

"I am in doubt on that point. He is a rich man, but for all that he may have gone in beyond his means."

"I am sorry for him, but that was reckless."

"Yes, he was completely taken in by Wall. He's a smooth fellow."

Walter had listened with languid attention; still, however, gathering the meaning of what was said until the mention of his father's name roused him, and then he listened eagerly, and with a sudden quickening of the pulse. He instantly connected the idea of what he had heard with his father's sudden illness, and naturally associated the two together.

"My father has heard of the failure of the company, and that has made him sick," he thought.

Though this implied a double misfortune, it relieved his anxiety a little. It supplied a cause for his father's illness. He had been afraid that his father had met with some accident, perhaps of a fatal nature. But if he had become ill in consequence of heavy losses, it was not likely that the illness was a very severe one.

He thought of speaking to the gentlemen, and making some further inquiries about the Mining Company and Mr. James Wall, but it occurred to him that his father might not like to have him pry into his affairs, and he therefore refrained.

When the gentlemen left the cars, he saw one of them had left a morning paper lying in the seat. He picked it up, and examined the columns until his eyes fell upon the following paragraph:—

"The failure of the Great Metropolitan Mining Company proves to be a disastrous one. The assets will not be sufficient to pay more than five per cent. of the amount of the sums invested by the stockholders, possibly not that. There must have been gross mismanagement somewhere, or such a result could hardly have been reached. We understand that the affairs of the company are in the hands of assignees who are empowered to wind them up. The stockholders in this vicinity will await the result with anxiety."

"That looks rather discouraging, to be sure," thought Walter. "I suppose father will lose a good deal. But I'll tell him he needn't worry about me. I shan't mind being poor, even if it comes to that. As long as he is left to me, I won't complain."

Walter became comparatively cheerful. He felt convinced that loss of property was all that was to be apprehended, and with the elastic spirits of youth he easily reconciled himself to that. He had never had occasion to think much about money. All his wants had been provided for with a lavish hand. He had, of course, seen poor people, but he did not realize what poverty meant. He had even thought at times that it must be rather a pleasant thing to earn one's own living. Still he did not apprehend that he would have to do this. His father might have lost heavily, but probably not to such an extent as to render this necessary.

So the time passed until, about half-past eleven o'clock, the cars stopped at Willoughby station.

The station was in rather a lonely spot,—that is, no houses were very near. Walter did not stop to speak to anybody, but, on leaving the cars, carpet-bag in hand, jumped over a fence, and took his way across the fields to his father's house. By the road it would have been a mile, but it was scarcely more than half a mile by the foot-path.

So it happened that he reached home without meeting a single person. He went up the door-way to the front door and rang the bell.

The door was opened by Nancy Forbes, the house-keeper, whose name was appended to the telegram.

"So it's you, Master Walter," she said. "I am glad you are home, but it's a sad home you're come to."

"Is father *very* sick, then?" asked Walter, turning pale.

"Didn't anybody tell you, then?"

"Tell me what?"

"My dear child, your father died at eight o'clock this morning."

CHAPTER III. AT HOME.

It was a terrible shock to Walter,—this sudden announcement of his father's death. When he had left home, Mr. Conrad seemed in his usual health, and he could not realize that he was dead. The news stunned him, and he stood, pale and motionless, looking into the house-keeper's face.

"Come in, Master Walter, come in, and have a cup of hot tea. It'll make you feel better."

A cup of hot tea was Nancy's invariable remedy for all troubles, physical or mental.

"Tell me about it, Nancy; I—I can't think it's true. It's so sudden."

"That's the way I feel too, Master Walter. And only yesterday morning, too, he looked just as usual. Little did I think what was to be."

"When was he first taken sick?"

Walter had seated himself on a chair in the hall, and waited anxiously for an answer.

"I didn't notice nothing till last night just after supper. Richard went to the post-office and got your father's letters. When they came he took 'em into the library, and began to read them. There was three, I remember. It was about an hour before I went into the room to tell him the carpenter had called about repairing the carriage-house. When I came in, there lay your poor father on the carpet, senseless. He held a letter tight in his hand. I screamed for help. Mr. Brier, the carpenter, and Richard came in and helped me to lift up your poor father, and we sent right off for the doctor."

"What did the doctor say?"

"He said it was a paralytic stroke,—a very bad one,—and ordered him to be put to bed directly. But it was of no use. He never recovered, but breathed his last this morning at eight o'clock. The doctor told me I must telegraph to your teacher;

and so I did."

"Nancy, have you got that letter which my father was reading?"

"Yes, Master Walter, I put it in my pocket without reading. I think there must have been bad news in it."

She drew from her pocket a letter, which she placed in Walter's hands. He read it hastily, and it confirmed his suspicions. It was from a lawyer Mr. Conrad had asked to make inquiries respecting the Great Metropolitan Mining Company, and was as follows:—

"William Conrad, Esq.

"Dear Sir:—I have, at your request, taken pains to inform myself of the present management and condition of the Great Metropolitan Mining Company. The task has been less difficult than I anticipated, since the failure of the company has just been made public. The management has been in the hands of dishonest and unscrupulous men, and it is doubtful whether the stockholders will be able to recover anything.

"Hoping you are not largely interested, I remain,
"Yours, very respectfully,
"Andrew Holmes."

Walter re-folded the letter, and put it into his pocket. He felt that this letter had cost his father his life, and in the midst of his grief he could not help thinking bitterly of the unscrupulous man who had led his father to ruin. Had it been merely the loss of property, he could have forgiven him, but he had been deprived of the kindest and most indulgent of fathers.

"I should like to see my father," he said.

We will not accompany him into the dark chamber where his father lay, unobservant, for the first time, of his presence. Such a scene is too sacred to be described.

An hour later he came out of the chamber, pale but

composed. He seemed older and more thoughtful than when he entered. A great and sudden sorrow often has this effect upon the young.

"Nancy," he said, "have any arrangements been made about the funeral?"

"No, Walter, we waited till you came. Mr. Edson will be here in a few minutes, and you can speak with him about it."

Mr. Edson, though not a professional undertaker, usually acted as such whenever there was occasion for his services. When he arrived, Walter requested him to take entire charge of the funeral.

"Are there any directions you would like to give, Walter?" asked Mr. Edson, who, like most of the villagers, had known Walter from his birth.

"No, Mr. Edson, I leave all to you."

"What relations are there to be invited?"

"My father had no near relatives. There is a cousin, Jacob Drummond, who lives in Stapleton. It will be necessary to let him know."

"Would a letter reach him in time?"

"It will be best to telegraph. Stapleton is forty miles distant, and it is doubtful if a letter would reach there in time."

"If you will write the telegram, Walter, I'll see that it's sent right off."

"I won't trouble you, Mr. Edson; you will have enough to attend to, and I can send Richard to the telegraph office, or go myself. I shall feel better for the exercise."

"Very well, Walter, I will do whatever else is necessary."

CHAPTER IV. JACOB DRUMMOND, OF STAPLETON.

Jacob Drummond kept a dry-goods store in the village of Stapleton. As the village was of considerable size, and he had no competitors, he drove a flourishing trade, and had already acquired quite a comfortable property. In fact, even had he been less favorably situated, he was pretty sure to thrive. He knew how to save money better, even, than to earn it, being considered, and with justice, a very mean man. He carried his meanness not only into his business, but into his household, and there was not a poor mechanic in Stapleton, and scarcely a poor laborer, who did not live better than Mr. Drummond, who was the rich man of the place.

No one, to look at Jacob Drummond, would have been likely to mistake his character. All the lines of his face, the expression of his thin lips, his cold gray eyes, all bespoke his meanness. Poor Mrs. Drummond, his wife, could have testified to it, had she dared; but in this house, at least, the husband was master, and she dared not express the opinions she secretly entertained of the man to whom she was bound for life.

At five o'clock on the afternoon of the day after Mr. Conrad's death, Mr. Drummond entered the house, which was on the opposite side of the street from the store.

This was the supper hour, and supper was ready upon the table.

A single glance was sufficient to show that Mr. Drummond was not a man to indulge in luxurious living. There was a plate of white bread, cut in thin slices, a small plate of butter, half a pie, and a plate of cake. A small pitcher of milk, a bowl of coarse brown sugar, and a pot of the cheapest kind of tea completed the preparations for the evening meal. Certainly there was nothing extravagant about these preparations; but Mr. Drummond thought otherwise. His attention was at once drawn to the cake, and instantly a frown gathered upon his face.

"Are we going to have company to-night, Mrs. Drummond?" he asked.

"Not that I know of," answered his wife, in some surprise.

"Then why is it that you have put both pie and cake on the table?"

"There was only half a pie, Mr. Drummond," said she, nervously.

"Well, there are but three of us. You can get three good-sized pieces from half a pie. That will be one for each of us. What would you have more?"

"The cake is a cheap kind."

"No cake is cheap, Mrs. Drummond. I take it you used eggs, butter, and sugar in making it."

"Yes, but—"

"No buts, if you please, Mrs. Drummond. You are probably not aware that all these articles are very dear at present. Until they get lower we need not have cake, except when company is present."

That being the case, Mr. Drummond was not likely to be put to much expense on this score. They seldom had company, and those who came once were not anxious to come again. For even on such occasions Mr. Drummond could not forget his ruling principle. The overflowing hospitality which even in the humblest village households crowns the board with plenty when visitors are present, was never to be found there; and, besides, the visitors could not help having an uneasy suspicion that their host grudged them the niggardly entertainment he did provide. So for three years the Stapleton Sewing Circle had met but once at the Drummonds', and there was no immediate prospect of their meeting there for another three years.

It may be supposed that Mr. Drummond was not fond of good eating. This, however, would be quite a mistake. When he dined or took tea out, he always did full justice to the different dainties which were provided, and quite seemed to enjoy them as long as they were furnished at the expense of another.

"Take away the cake, if you please, Mrs. Drummond," continued her husband. "You can save it for Sunday evening."

"I am afraid it will be dried up by that time."

"If it is dry, you can steam it."

"That spoils cake."

"You seem very contrary to-night, Mrs. Drummond. I have continually to check you in your extravagant tastes. Cake and pie, indeed! If you had your way, you would double my household expenses."

Mrs. Drummond rose from the table, and meekly removed the offending cake.

Just then the third and only other member of the family entered.

This was Joshua Drummond, the only son, now eighteen years of age, though he looked scarcely more than sixteen. He inherited his father's meanness, but not his frugality. He was more self-indulgent, and, though he grudged spending money for others, was perfectly ready to spend as much as he could get hold of for himself.

CHAPTER V. JACOB DRUMMOND—CONTINUED.

Over Joshua Mr. Drummond had less control than over his wife. The latter gave way meekly to his unreasonable requisitions; but Joshua did not hesitate to make opposition, being as selfish and self-willed as his father, for whom he entertained neither respect nor affection.

Joshua looked around him disdainfully.

"Is this Fast Day?" he asked.

"You know very well that Fast Day comes in April," said his father.

"I only judged from the looks of the table," said Joshua, not very respectfully. "You don't mean that we shall any of us suffer from the gout."

"Bread and butter and pie are good enough for anybody," said Mr. Drummond, stiffly.

"I don't see any pie. Excuse me, there is a little,—so little that I did not at first see it."

This was too much for Mr. Drummond's temper.

"Unmannerly boy!" he exclaimed; "if you are dissatisfied with the fare you get at home, you can engage board elsewhere."

"I would like to," muttered Joshua, in a low voice, which his father chose not to hear.

In silence he helped himself to bread and butter, and in due time accepted a piece of pie, which Mrs. Drummond made larger at the expense of her own share.

Harmony thus being restored, Mr. Drummond remarked, "I've had a telegram to-day from Willoughby."

"From Willoughby?" repeated his wife. "Isn't that where your cousin William Conrad lives?"

"He doesn't live there any longer. He's dead."

"Dead! When did he die?"

"I don't know. Yesterday, I suppose. The funeral is to be day after to-morrow."

"Shall you go?"

"Yes. It will cost me considerable; as much as five dollars or more; but he was my cousin, and it is my duty to go," said Mr. Drummond, with the air of a man who was making a great sacrifice.

"He was rich, wasn't he?" asked Joshua, becoming interested.

"Probably worth a hundred thousand dollars," said his father, complacently.

"I should think he might have left me something," said Joshua.

"He never saw you, Joshua," said his mother.

"Joshua stands a better chance of getting a legacy from one who doesn't know him, than from one who does," said Mr. Drummond, with grim pleasantry.

"He leaves children, doesn't he, Mr. Drummond?"

"One child—a boy. Let me see, he must be fifteen by this time."

"And his mother isn't living?"

"No."

"Poor boy!"

"He'll be a rich boy, Mrs. Drummond, and I'll tell you what, I shouldn't wonder if we had a good chance to know him."

"How so?"

"It's likely I will be appointed his guardian. I'm the nearest relative, so that will be the most proper course."

"Will he come here, then?" asked Joshua.

"Very probably."

"Then I hope you'll live better, or he won't stand it."

"When I require any advice from you, Joshua, I will apply for it," said his father.

Joshua inwardly hoped that his father would be appointed guardian, as it might make a difference in the family living; and, besides, if his cousin were rich, he meant to wheedle himself into his confidence, in the hope of future advantage.

"When shall you set out?" asked Mrs. Drummond.

"To-morrow morning, I think," said her husband. "It will be hard to leave, but it's due to my cousin's memory."

Mr. Drummond had become very punctilious all at once, considering that for the last dozen years Mr. Conrad, who had by no means admired him, had had little or no communication with him. But then he had died rich, and who knows what sort of a will he had left? At any rate, Jacob began to feel a strong interest in him now. He might have put off going to Willoughby till the morning train on the day of the funeral, for two o'clock was the hour fixed for the last ceremony; but he was in a hurry to learn all he could about the property, and secure, if possible, the guardianship for himself. This was the secret of his willingness to sacrifice time and money out of regard to his cousin's memory. The next day, therefore, he started, taking with him in his valise a lunch of bread and meat tied up in a piece of brown paper. He didn't intend to spend any more money than was absolutely necessary on tavern bills.

Shortly after his arrival, he called at the house of mourning.

"I am Jacob Drummond, of Stapleton, the cousin of the deceased," he explained to Nancy, who opened the door to admit him. "Is my young relative, Mr. Conrad's son, at home?"

"Yes, sir," said Nancy, taking an inventory of his features, and deciding that he was a very disagreeable looking man.

"Will you mention my name to him, and say that I should like to see him?"

Mr. Drummond was ushered into the parlor, where he had a little chance to look around him before Walter appeared.

"It's all nonsense wasting so much money on furniture," he mentally ejaculated. "The money spent is a dead loss when it might be drawing handsome interest."

Walter did not long keep him waiting.

Mr. Drummond rose at his entrance.

"I suppose you don't know me," he said; "but I was your father's nearest living relation."

"Mr. Drummond, I believe."

"Yes, Jacob Drummond, of Stapleton. You have probably heard your father speak of me?"

"Yes, sir," said Walter.

"I came as soon as I could after getting the telegram. I left my business to take care of itself. I wanted to offer you my sympathy on your sad loss."

Mr. Drummond's words were kind, though the reference to his sacrifice in leaving his business might have been as well left out. Still Walter could not feel as grateful as he wanted to do. Somehow he didn't fancy Mr. Drummond.

"You are very kind," he said.

"I mean to be. You know I'm your nearest relation now. I truly feel for you in your desolate condition, and though it may not be the right time to say it, I must tell you that I hope, when the funeral is over, you will accompany me home, and share our humble hospitality. Mrs. Drummond joins with me in the invitation."

Mrs. Drummond had not been consulted in the matter, but her husband thought it would sound well to say so.

"I have not had time to think of future arrangements," said Walter; "but I thank you for your invitation."

Walter did not know the motives which induced Mr. Drummond to extend this invitation, but supposed it to be meant in kindness, and so acknowledged it.

"My son Joshua, too," said Mr. Drummond, "is longing to make your acquaintance. He is older than you, but not much larger. How old are you?"

"I am fifteen."

"You are well grown of your age; Joshua is eighteen, but

he will make a very pleasant companion for you. Let me hope that you will accept my invitation."

"Thank you, Mr. Drummond; I will consult my friends about it."

"I wonder how much board I could venture to ask," thought Mr. Drummond. "If I am his guardian, I can fix that to suit myself. A hundred thousand dollars would make me a rich man. That is, I could make money from it, without injuring the boy."

Mr. Drummond asked a few more questions about Mr. Conrad's sickness and death. Walter answered them, but did not think it necessary to speak of his losses by the Mining Company. Mr. Drummond was a stranger, and not a man to inspire confidence. So Walter told as little as he could. At length the visitor, having exhausted inquiries, rose.

"I shall be here to-morrow," he said. "I am stopping at the tavern. I shall return to Stapleton after the ceremony. I hope you will make up your mind to go back with me."

"I could not be ready so soon," answered Walter, doubtfully.

"I can wait till the next day."

"That will not be necessary, Mr. Drummond. I shall have no difficulty in making the journey alone, if I conclude to accept your kind invitation."

Mr. Drummond shook our hero's hand sympathetically, and at length withdrew. As he went down the avenue, he took a backward glance at the handsome mansion in which his cousin had lived.

"That boy owns all that property," he said, half enviously, "and never worked a day for it. I've had to work for all my money. But it was foolish to spend so much money on a house. A third the sum would have built a comfortable house, and the rest might have been put at interest. If it turns out that I am the boy's guardian, I think I shall sell it. That'll be the best course."

With these reflections Mr. Drummond pursued his way back to the village tavern, where he had taken the precaution to ascertain that he should be charged but a dollar and a quarter a day. He considered that a dollar would have been sufficient, but still it was proper to make some sacrifice to his cousin's memory. Mr. Conrad's mining speculation was not generally known in the village as yet, so that Mr. Drummond did not hear a word as to his loss of property.

CHAPTER VI. FUTURE PLANS.

The funeral was over. Mr. Drummond, as indeed his relationship permitted, was one of the principal mourners. Considering that he had not seen Mr. Conrad for five years preceding his death, nor during that time communicated with him in any way, he appeared to be very much overcome by grief. He kept his eyes covered with a large white handkerchief, and his movements indicated suppressed agitation. He felt that this was a tribute due to a cousin who had left over one hundred thousand dollars.

When they had returned from the grave, Mr. Drummond managed to have a word with Walter.

"Have you decided to accept my offer, and make your home beneath my humble roof?" he asked.

"There has been no time to consult with my friends here, Mr. Drummond. I will let you know next week. I thank you at any rate for your kindness."

"Do come, Walter," said his cousin, twisting his mean features into an affectionate smile. "With you beneath my humble roof, I shall want nothing to complete my happiness."

Walter thanked him again, wondering at the same time why Mr. Drummond's kindness did not affect him more sensibly.

So Jacob Drummond went back to Stapleton, still ignorant of the state of Mr. Conrad's affairs, and still regarding Walter as a boy of great wealth.

When the will was opened it was found to bear date two years back, before Mr. Conrad had plunged into the speculation which had proved so disastrous to him. He bequeathed all the property which he did possess to Walter, with the exception of five hundred dollars, which were left as a legacy to his faithful house-keeper, Nancy Forbes. At the time the will was made, its provisions made Walter heir to a large fortune. Now it was quite uncertain how things would turn out. Clement Shaw, the village lawyer, an honest and upright man, was made executor, being an old and tried friend of the deceased.

With him Walter had a long and confidential conversation, imparting to him what he knew of his father's mining speculation and its disastrous result, with its probable effect in accelerating his death.

"I knew something of this before, Walter," said Mr. Shaw. "Your father spoke to me of being largely interested in the Great Metropolitan Mining Company; but of the company itself and the extent to which he was involved I knew nothing."

"I think my father must have been very seriously involved," said Walter. "It may, perhaps, swallow up the whole property."

"Let us hope not. Indeed, I can hardly believe that your father would have ventured in so deep as that."

"He had every confidence in the company; he thought he was going to double his money. If only a part of his property was threatened, I don't think it would have had such an effect upon him."

"I will thoroughly examine into the affair," said Mr. Shaw. "Meanwhile, Walter, hope for the best! It can hardly be that the whole property is lost. Do not be too anxious."

"Do not fear for me on that account," said Walter. "I always looked forward to being rich, it is true, but I can bear poverty. If the worst comes, and I am penniless, I am strong, and can work. I can get along as well as thousands of other boys, who have to support themselves."

Walter did not speak boastfully, but in a calm, confident way, that argued a consciousness of power.

"Yes," said the lawyer, regarding him attentively, "I think you are right there. You are just the boy who can make his own way; but I hope you will not be obliged to do so."

"There is one thing I want to say, Mr. Shaw," said Walter, "and that is about the money my father leaves in his will to

Nancy."

"The circumstances were different. She will not expect it now; that is, of course, unless things turn out more favorably than we fear."

"That is not what I mean. Nancy must have the money, if there is so much left after settling the estate."

"But suppose only five hundred dollars are left? Of course I hope it will be much more, but we must think of all contingencies."

"If only five hundred dollars are left, let Nancy have them."

"But, Walter, consider yourself."

"I am young and strong. Nancy has spent her best years in my father's service, and she is no longer young. It is right that she should have some provision. Besides, my father meant her to have it, and I want to carry out his wishes."

"This is all very generous, Walter; but I am afraid it is inconsiderate. It would not be your father's wish to provide even for Nancy, however faithful she may have been, at the expense of his son."

"It is right," said Walter. "Besides, Mr. Shaw, I find that Nancy had laid up six hundred dollars, which she had deposited in my father's hands. That also must be paid, if there is enough to pay it; if not, I will take it upon myself to pay whenever I am able."

"You're an excellent boy, Walter," said Mr. Shaw. "I always had a good opinion of you, and I find it is more than deserved. I honor you for the resolution you have expressed, though I cannot quite agree with you about the five hundred dollars. As to the debt, that must be paid, if there is money enough to pay it. But we can leave the further discussion of this question for the present. Now let us consider what is to become of you in the mean time. You were at the Essex Classical

Institute, I believe?"

"Yes, sir."

"You would like to go back again, I suppose."

"No, Mr. Shaw. It is an expensive school, and while it is uncertain how my father's affairs will come out, I should not feel justified in going there."

"Perhaps you are right. Of course you cannot stay here, and keep house by yourself. I would invite you to my own house, but my wife is an invalid, and I have to consider her in the matter."

"Thank you, Mr. Shaw; but I think perhaps I had better accept the offer of Mr. Drummond, of Stapleton. He invites me to make my home at his house, and, for the present, perhaps, that will be the best arrangement."

"I am not acquainted with Mr. Drummond. He is a relation, I believe."

"Yes, he is my father's cousin, and so, of course, my second cousin."

"I think I saw him at the funeral."

"Yes, he was present."

Mr. Shaw had seen Jacob Drummond, and had not been very favorably impressed by his appearance. Still, his offer was not one to be hastily rejected, for no better reason than a little prejudice, which might prove unfounded. Accordingly he said, "Well, Walter, as you say, I am not sure whether this may not be the best arrangement for you, that is, for the present. If you don't like to stay at Stapleton, you can write me, and I will see what I can do for you."

"Thank you, Mr. Shaw."

Nancy was much troubled at the thought of parting from Walter, whom she had known from his infancy; but a situation was immediately offered her in the village, and Walter promised to take her as his house-keeper whenever he had a home of his own, and this comforted her, although it was likely to be a long time first, since our hero was at present but fifteen.

"Your six hundred dollars shall be paid, Nancy," said Walter, "as soon as father's affairs are settled."

"Don't bother yourself about that, Master Walter," said Nancy. "I've got fifty dollars in my trunk, and I don't need the other at all. I can wait for it five years."

"It won't be necessary to wait as long as that, Nancy."

"And so you are going to that Mr. Drummond's? I'm sorry for it. I don't like the man's looks at all."

"He may be a good man. He was kind to invite me."

"He isn't a good man," said Nancy, positively. "He's got a mean sort of look to his face."

"You mustn't try to prejudice me before I go to him, Nancy."

"You'll think as I do before you've been there a week," said Nancy, shaking her head. "I took a good look at him when he was here, and I didn't like his looks."

"He isn't very handsome," said Walter, smiling; "but everybody can't be handsome."

Secretly he did not wonder much at Nancy's prejudice. Mr. Drummond certainly was a mean-looking man. How he could be so nearly related to his father, who was a generous, open-handed, and open-hearted man, was surprising. Still Walter was just enough to reserve his judgment until his opportunities of judging were greater than at present.

He wrote a brief letter to Stapleton, to the following effect:—

"Mr. Drummond:—

"Dear Sir:—I will accept the invitation you were kind enough to extend to me, for the present, at least, and will come to Stapleton about the middle of next week. You are the only relation of my father that I know of, and I think it would be his wish that I should go to you. If it should be inconvenient for you to receive me at that time, please write me at once.

"Yours, respectfully,
"Walter Conrad."

In return, Walter received a letter couched in the most cordial terms, in which Mr. Drummond signed himself, "Your affectionate cousin." He was delighted, he said, to think that he was about to receive, under his humble roof, the son of his revered and lamented cousin.

CHAPTER VII. MR. DRUMMOND'S HUMBLE ROOF.

"Mrs. Drummond," said her husband, "young Mr. Conrad will be here by four o'clock this afternoon. You will have a nice supper ready at five."

"Shall I have cake and pie both?" inquired Mrs. Drummond, doubtfully.

"Certainly. Indeed, it may be as well to have two kinds of pie, say apple and pumpkin; and, as we have not had hot biscuit for some time, you may bake some."

Mrs. Drummond looked at her husband as if she had doubts as to his sanity. Such a luxurious meal was quite unheard of in the Drummond household.

"Cake, two kinds of pie, and hot biscuit!" she repeated.

"Yes," he replied. "I am not in general in favor of such extra living, but it is well to pay some respect to the memory of my deceased kinsman in the person of his son. Being the son of a rich man, he has been accustomed to rich living, and I wish him, on his advent into our family, to feel at home."

Mrs. Drummond prepared to obey her husband's directions with alacrity.

"Joshua will get a good supper for once," she thought, thinking more of her son than of the stranger who was to enter the family. "How surprised he will be to see such a variety on the table!"

Not that Joshua was strictly confined to the spare diet of his father's table. Through his mother's connivance there was generally an extra piece of pie or cake in the pantry laid aside for him. Had Mr. Drummond suspected this, he would have been very angry; but, being at the store the greater portion of the time, he was not aware of the extra indulgence.

Mr. Drummond himself met Walter at the depot.

"I am delighted to welcome you to Stapleton, my young friend," he said, shaking his hand cordially. "In the affliction which has come upon you, let me hope that you will find a haven of rest beneath my humble roof."

"I wonder why he always speaks of his 'humble roof,'" thought Walter. "Does he live in a shanty, I wonder?"

He made suitable acknowledgments, and proceeded to walk beside Mr. Drummond to the house which he termed humble.

It did not deserve that name, being a substantial two-story house, rather ugly architecturally, but comfortable enough in appearance.

"That is my humble dwelling," said Mr. Drummond, pointing it out. "It is not equal to the splendid mansion in which you have been accustomed to live, for my worldly circumstances differ widely from those of your late lamented parent; but I trust that in our humble way we shall be enabled to make you comfortable."

"Thank you, Mr. Drummond; I have no doubt of that. Your house looks very comfortable."

"Yes, it is plain and humble, but comfortable. We are plain people. We are not surrounded by the appliances of wealth, but we manage, in our humble way, to get through life. That is my son Joshua, who is looking out of the front window. I hope you may become good friends, considering how nearly you are related."

Walter raised his eyes, and saw Joshua, whose small, mean features, closely resembling his father's, expressed considerable curiosity. Walter secretly doubted whether he should like him; but this doubt he kept to himself.

Mr. Drummond opened the outer door, and led the way in.

"This is my wife, Mrs. Drummond," he said, as she approached, and kindly welcomed the young stranger.

"I think I shall like her," thought Walter, suffering his glance to rest for a moment on her mild, placid features; "she is evidently quite superior to her husband."

"Joshua, come here and welcome Mr. Conrad," said his father.

Joshua came forward awkwardly, and held out his hand with the stiffness of a pump-handle.

"How dy do?" he said. "Just come?"

"Yes," said Walter, accepting the hand, and shaking it slightly.

"Are you tired with your journey, Mr. Conrad?" asked Mrs. Drummond. "Perhaps you would like to be shown to your room."

"Thank you," said Walter. "I will go up for a few minutes."

"Where are you going to put our young friend, Mrs. Drummond?"

"In the spare chamber."

"That is right. You will find some difference, Mr. Conrad, between our humble accommodations and the sumptuous elegance of your own home; but we will try and make it up by a hearty welcome."

"I wish he wouldn't use the word *humble* so much," thought Walter.

Walter went upstairs, preceded by Mr. Drummond, who insisted on carrying his carpet-bag, for his trunk would not arrive till the next day, having been forwarded by express.

"I say, mother," remarked Joshua, "the old man's awfully polite to this young fellow."

"You shouldn't speak of your father in that way, Joshua."

"Oh, what's the odds? He is an old man, isn't he? I just wish he'd be as polite to me. I say, I hope he'll like his boarding-place. What are you going to have for supper?"

"Hot biscuit, cake, and two kinds of pie."

"Whew! won't the old man look like a thundercloud?"

"That's what he told me to get. You do your father

injustice, Joshua."

Mrs. Drummond knew in her secret heart that her husband was intensely mean; but she was one of those who like to think as well as possible of every one, and was glad of an opportunity to prove that he could, on rare occasions, be more generous.

"Father's brain must be softening," said Joshua, after recovering in a measure from his astonishment. "I hope it will be permanent. Isn't supper most ready?"

"At five o'clock, Joshua."

"This young chap's got a lot of money, I suppose, and the governor's after some of it. That explains the matter."

"I wish you wouldn't speak so disrespectfully of your father, Joshua."

"I won't if he'll keep on as he's begun. I'm glad this young Conrad has come to board here. I'm going to get thick with him."

"He seems like a very nice boy," said Mrs. Drummond.

"I don't care what sort of a boy he is, as long as he's got the tin. I'm going to make him treat."

"You must be considerate of his feelings, Joshua. Remember that he has just lost his father."

"Suppose he has, there's no need of looking glum about it."

Had Jacob Drummond died, Joshua would have borne the loss with the greatest fortitude. Of that there was no doubt. Indeed, he would rather have hailed the event with joy, if, as he expressed it, the "old man did the right thing," and left him the bulk of his property. Though such feelings did not do Joshua much credit, it must be said in extenuation that his father was far from being a man to inspire affection in any one, however nearly related.

At five o'clock they sat down to supper.

"I hope, Mr. Conrad," said Jacob, "you will be able to relish our humble repast."

"Humble again!" thought Walter. He was about to say that everything looked very nice, when Joshua broke in.

"If you call this humble, I don't know what you'd say to the suppers we commonly have."

Mr. Drummond, who desired, for this day, at least, to keep up appearances, frowned with vexation.

"Joshua," he said, "I desire that you will act in a more gentlemanly way, or else leave the table."

As leaving the table on the present occasion would have been, indeed, a deprivation, Joshua thought it wise not to provoke his father too far, at any rate until after he had made sure of his supper. He therefore left most of the conversation to his father.

"Have you ever been in Stapleton before, Mr. Conrad?" asked Mr. Drummond.

"No, sir; never."

"It is not a large place, but it is growing; the people are plain, but they have kind hearts. I hope you may like the town after a while."

"Thank you, sir; I have no doubt I shall."

"If you feel inclined for a walk, Joshua will go out with you after supper, and show you the mill-dam, the church, and the school-house. He will also point out the store—it is only across the way—where, in my humble way, I try to earn a living. I shall be very glad if you will come in and take a look inside. I may be busy, for work has accumulated during my absence, but Joshua will show you around."

"Thank you, sir."

"Will you have another cup of tea, Mr. Conrad?" asked Mrs. Drummond.

"Thank you."

"May I ask, Mr. Conrad,—excuse my intruding the question,—who is left executor of your father's estate?"

"Mr. Shaw, the lawyer in our village."

"Is he? Do you have confidence in him?"

"He is an excellent man, very honest and upright. He was an intimate friend of my father."

"Ah, indeed! I am glad of it. Then he will consult your interests."

"Yes, sir, I feel quite safe in his hands."

"I am so glad to hear you say so. So many lawyers, you know, are tricky."

"Mr. Shaw is not tricky."

"We have no lawyer here," pursued Mr. Drummond. "You will perhaps be surprised to hear it, but my humble services are frequently called into requisition, in administering and settling estates."

"Indeed, sir."

"Yes; but I am glad you have got a man you can trust. Mrs. Drummond, I think Mr. Conrad will have another piece of pie."

Supper was over at length, and Walter, by invitation, went out to walk with Joshua.

CHAPTER VIII. WALTER MAKES A REVELATION.

Walter did not anticipate a very pleasant walk with Joshua. The little he had seen of that young man did not prepossess him in his favor. However, having no other way of spending his time, he had no objection to the walk.

"That's the old man's store just across the street," said Joshua, as they emerged from the house.

"Your father's?"

"Of course. Don't you see the name on the sign?" Walter did see it, but never having been accustomed to speak of his own father as "the old man," he was not quite sure he apprehended Joshua's meaning.

"You were an only child, weren't you?" said Joshua.

"Yes," said Walter, soberly.

Illustration

He could not help thinking what a comfort it would have been to him to have either brother or sister. He would have felt less alone in the world.

"So am I," said Joshua; adding, complacently, "Between you and I, the old man has laid up quite a snug sum. Of course it'll all come to me some day."

"I am glad to hear it," said Walter, rather wondering that Joshua should have made such a communication to a comparative stranger.

"To hear the old man talk," pursued Joshua, "you'd think he was awful poor. He's stingy enough about everything in the house. There isn't a family in town that don't live better than we do."

"I thought we had a very good supper," said Walter, who experienced not a little disgust at Joshua's charges against his father.

"That was because you were with us. The old man laid himself out for the occasion."

"I am sorry if any difference was made on my account."

"Well, I aint. It's the first decent supper I've eaten at home since the Sewing Circle met at our house three years ago."

"Is that the church?" asked Walter, desirous of diverting the conversation into another channel.

"Yes, that's the old meeting-house. I hate to go there. The minister's an old fogy."

"What is that I see through the trees? Is it a river?"

"No, it's a pond."

"Do you ever go out on it?"

"Not very often. I tried to get the old man to buy me a boat, but he wouldn't do it. He's too stingy."

"I wouldn't talk so about your father."

"Why not?"

"Because he is entitled to your respect."

"I don't know about that. If he'd treat me as he ought to, I'd treat him accordingly. He never gives me a cent if he can help it. Now how much do you think he allows me a week for spending money?"

"I can't tell."

"Only fifty cents, and I'm eighteen years old. Isn't that mean?"

"It isn't a very large sum."

"Of course not. He ought to give me five dollars a week, and then I'd buy my own clothes. Now I have to take up with what I can get. He wanted to have his old overcoat, that he'd worn three winters, made over for me; but I wouldn't stand it. I told him I'd go without first."

Though these communications did not raise Joshua in the estimation of Walter, the latter could not help thinking that there was probably some foundation for what was said, and the prejudice against Mr. Drummond, for which he had blamed himself as without cause, began to find some extenuation.

"When I talk to the old man about his stinting me so,"

continued Joshua, "he tells me to go to work and earn some money."

"Why don't you do it?"

"He wants me to go into his store, but he wouldn't pay me anything. He offered me a dollar and a half a week; but I wasn't going to work ten or twelve hours a day for no such sum. If I could get a light, easy place in the city, say at ten dollars a week, I'd go. There aint any chance in Stapleton for a young man of enterprise."

"I've thought sometimes," said Walter, "that I should like to get a place in the city; but I suppose I couldn't get enough at first to pay my board."

"You get a place!" exclaimed Joshua, in astonishment. "I thought you was going to college."

"Father intended I should; but his death will probably change my plans."

"I don't see why."

"It is expensive passing through college; I cannot afford it."

"Oh, that's all humbug. You're talking like the old man."

"How do you know that it is humbug?" demanded Walter, not very well pleased with his companion's tone.

"Why, you're rich. The old man told me that your father left a hundred thousand dollars. You're the only son; you told me so yourself."

"Your father is mistaken."

"What, wasn't your father rich?" asked Joshua, opening his small eyes in amazement.

"My father was unfortunate enough to get involved in a speculation, by which he lost heavily. I can't tell how his affairs stand till they are settled. I may be left penniless."

"Do you mean that?" asked Joshua, stopping short and facing his companion.

"I generally mean what I say," said Walter, rather stiffly.

Joshua's answer was a low whistle of amazement.

"Whew!" he said. "That's the biggest joke I've heard of lately;" and he followed up this remark by a burst of merriment.

Walter surveyed him with surprise. He certainly did not know what to make of Joshua's conduct.

"I don't see any joke about it," he said. "I don't complain of being poor, for I think I can earn my own living; but it doesn't strike me as a thing to laugh at."

"I was laughing to think how the old man is taken in. It's rich!"

Joshua burst into another fit of boisterous laughter.

"How is he taken in?"

"He thinks you're worth a hundred thousand dollars," said Joshua, going off in another peal of merriment.

"Well, he is mistaken, that's all. I don't see how he is taken in."

"He's been doing the polite, and treating you as if you was a prince of the blood. That's the reason he told the old woman to get up such a nice supper, he expected to get you to take him for a guardian, and then he'd have the handling of your money. Won't he be mad when he finds out how he's been taken in? Giving you the best room too! Are you sure that none of the property will be left?"

"Probably not much."

That Walter listened with mortification and disgust to what Joshua had told him about his father's selfish designs, is only what might be expected. It is always disagreeable to find out the meanness of those whom you have supposed kind to you for your own sake. This, to Walter, who had been accustomed to an atmosphere of kindness, was a painful discovery. It was his first experience of the coldness and hollowness of the world, and to the sensitive nature of youth this first revelation is very painful and very bitter.

"I am sorry to think that your father made such a

mistake," he said, coldly. "I will take care to undeceive him."

"What! You're not going to tell him, are you?"

"Certainly. I meant to do so; but I did not suppose he invited me just because he thought I was rich."

"What for, then?"

"Being my father's cousin and nearest relation, it didn't seem very strange that he should have invited me on that account."

"The old man's a shrewd one," said Joshua, rather admiringly. "He knows which way his bread is buttered. He don't lay himself out for no poor relations, not if he knows it."

"I am sorry if he has laid himself out for me under a mistake."

"I aint. It's a good joke on the old man. Besides, we all got a better supper by it. Don't you tell him about it till to-morrow."

"Why not?"

"Because, if you do, we'll have a mean breakfast as usual. I just want him to think you're rich a little while longer, so we can have something decent for once."

"I don't feel willing to deceive your father any longer. I have not willingly deceived him at all."

"You're a fool then!"

"Look here," said Walter, flushing a little, "I don't allow anybody to call me by that name."

"No offence," said Joshua, whose physical courage was not very great. "I didn't mean anything, of course, except that it was foolish to blurt it all out to-night, when there isn't any need of it. There isn't such an awful hurry, is there?"

"I would rather your father knew at once."

"To-morrow will be soon enough."

"At any rate I shall tell him to-morrow, then. But I've got tired walking. Suppose we go back."

"Just as you say."

They went back together. Mr. Drummond was in the store, but Mrs. Drummond was at home.

"You didn't go far," she said. "But I suppose you were tired, Mr. Conrad."

"A little," answered Walter.

"I wonder," thought our hero, "whether she will change as soon as she finds out that I am poor?" Somehow he felt that she would not. She seemed very different from her husband and son, and Walter was inclined to like her better.

Joshua went out again soon, not having much taste for staying at home; and, as Walter retired early, he did not see either him or his father again till the next morning at breakfast.

CHAPTER IX. HOW MR. DRUMMOND TOOK THE NEWS.

Joshua's anticipations of a good breakfast were realized. As he entered the room where the table was set, he saw a dish of beefsteak, another of fried potatoes, and some hot biscuit. This with coffee was very much better than the breakfast usually provided in the Drummond household.

Joshua burst into a fresh fit of laughter, thinking how his father had been taken in.

"What's the matter, Joshua?" asked his mother, who was the only one in the room besides himself.

"Oh, it's the richest joke, mother!"

"What is?" asked Mrs. Drummond, perplexed.

"I can't tell you now, but you'll find out pretty soon. Ho, ho!"

And Joshua commenced to laugh again.

"Has Mr. Conrad come downstairs?"

"I haven't seen Mr. Conrad this morning," answered Joshua, imitating his mother's tone in repeating the name.

Just then Walter entered, and said "Good-morning."

"Good-morning, Mr. Conrad," said Mrs. Drummond. "I hope you slept well."

"Very well, thank you," said Walter.

Mr. Drummond here entered from the street, having been for an hour in the store opposite.

"Good-morning, Mr. Conrad," he said. "I trust you rested well, and can do justice to our humble repast. I have been in the store an hour. We who are not endowed with the gifts of Fortune must be early astir."

Joshua tried to suppress a laugh, but not with entire success.

"What are you snickering at, Joshua?" demanded Mr. Drummond, in a displeased tone. "I don't know what Mr. Conrad will think of your manners."

"You'll excuse them, won't you, Mr. Conrad?" asked Joshua, beginning to chuckle again.

Knowing very well the source of his amusement, and feeling his own position to be an awkward one, Walter was all the more resolved to impart to Mr. Drummond without delay the posture of his father's affairs. He did not answer Joshua's appeal.

"I don't see what has got into you this morning, Joshua," said Mrs. Drummond, mildly. "You seem in very good spirits."

"So I am," said Joshua, with a grin.

His father suspected that the unusual excellence of the breakfast had something to do with Joshua's mirth, and was afraid he would let out something about it. This made him a little nervous, as he wanted to keep up appearances before his young guest.

Walter's appetite was not very good. His father's death weighed heavily upon him, and Joshua's revelation of the night before was not calculated to cheer him. It was mortifying to think that Mr. Drummond's gracious manner was entirely owing to his supposed wealth; but of this he entertained little doubt. He was anxious to have the truth known, no matter how unfavorably it might affect his position with the Drummonds. There were some, he knew, whose kindness did not depend on his reputed wealth. "You have a poor appetite, Mr. Conrad," said Mr. Drummond. "Let me give you another piece of steak."

"No, I thank you," said Walter.

"I'll take another piece, father," said Joshua.

"I have already helped you twice," said his father, frowning.

"I'm hungry this morning," said Joshua, who, knowing that he could not expect another as good breakfast, determined to do full justice to this.

"If you are, you need not overeat yourself," said Mr. Drummond, depositing on his son's outstretched plate a square inch of meat.

Joshua coolly helped himself to fried potatoes, and appropriated a hot biscuit, much to his father's annoyance. He resolved to give Joshua a private hint that he must be more sparing in his eating. He did not like to speak before Walter, desiring to keep up with him the character of a liberal man. Joshua understood his father's feelings, and it contributed to the enjoyment which he felt at the thought of how richly his father was sold.

At length breakfast was over.

"I must go back to the store," said Mr. Drummond. "Joshua will look after you, Mr. Conrad. I hope you will be able to pass the time pleasantly."

"If you can spare me five minutes, Mr. Drummond, I should like to speak to you in private," said Walter, determined to put an end to the misunderstanding at once.

"Certainly. I can spare five or ten minutes, or more, Mr. Conrad. Won't you walk into the parlor?"

The parlor was a very dreary-looking room, dark, cold, and cheerless. A carpet, of an ugly pattern, covered the floor; there was a centre-table in the middle of the room with a few books that were never opened resting upon it. Half-a-dozen cane-bottomed chairs stood about the room, and there were besides a few of the stock articles usually to be found in country parlors, including a very hard, inhospitable-looking sofa. As the Drummonds did not have much company, this room was very seldom used.

"Take a seat, Mr. Conrad," said Mr. Drummond, seating himself.

Mr. Drummond was far from anticipating the nature of Walter's communication. Indeed, he cherished a hope that our hero was about to ask his assistance in settling up the estate,—a request with which, it is needless to say, he would gladly have complied.

"I don't suppose you know how I am situated," Walter commenced. "I mean in relation to my father's estate."

"I suppose it was all left to you, and very properly. I congratulate you on starting in the world under such good auspices. I don't, of course, know how much your father left, but —"

"It is not certain that my father left anything," said Walter, thinking it best to reveal every thing at once.

"*What!*" exclaimed Mr. Drummond, his lower jaw falling, and looking very blank.

"My father made some investments recently that turned out badly."

"But he was worth a very large property,—it can't all be lost."

"I am afraid there will be very little left, if anything. He lost heavily by some mining stock, which he bought at a high figure, and which ran down to almost nothing."

"There's the house left, at any rate."

"My father borrowed its value, I understand; I am afraid that must go too."

Now, at length, it flashed upon Mr. Drummond how he had been taken in. He thought of the attentions he had lavished upon Walter, of the extra expense he had incurred, and all as it appeared for a boy likely to prove penniless. He might even expect to live upon him. These thoughts, which rapidly succeeded each other, mortified and made him angry.

"Why didn't you tell me this before, young man?" he demanded with asperity.

His change of tone and manner showed Walter that Joshua was entirely right in his estimate of his father's motives, and he in turn became indignant.

"When did you expect me to tell you, Mr. Drummond?"

he said quickly. "I only arrived yesterday afternoon, and I tell you this morning. I would have told you last night, if you had been in the house."

"Why didn't you tell me when I was at Willoughby?"

"I had other things to think of," said Walter, shortly. "The thought of my father's death and of my loss shut out everything else."

"Well, what are you going to do?" asked Mr. Drummond, in a hard tone.

"I shall have to earn my own living," said Walter. "I am well and strong, and am not afraid."

"That is a good plan," said Mr. Drummond, who knew Walter so little as to fear that he wanted to become dependent upon him.

"When I was of your age I had my own living to earn. What do you propose to do?"

"Have you a vacancy for me in your store? Joshua told me you wished him to go in."

"You couldn't earn much, for you don't know anything of the business."

"I should not expect to. I am perfectly willing to work for my board until I find out how my father's affairs are going to turn out."

This proposal struck Mr. Drummond favorably. He judged that Walter would prove a valuable assistant when he was broken in, for it was easy to see that he had energy. Besides, it was desirable to keep him near until it was decided whether Mr. Conrad's affairs were really in as bad a state as his son represented. Even if a few thousand dollars were left, Mr. Drummond would like the handling of that sum. Then, again, no one knew better than Mr. Drummond that Walter's board would cost him very little; for, of course, he would at once return to his usual frugal fare.

"Very well," he said; "you can go into the store on those terms. As you say, you've got your own living to earn, and the sooner you begin the better."

Walter had not said this, but he agreed with Mr. Drummond.

It may be thought strange that our hero should have been willing to enter the employment of such a mean man; but he thought it wisest to remain in the neighborhood until he could learn something definite about his father's affairs. He prepared to go to work at once, partly because he didn't wish to be dependent, partly because he foresaw that he should be happier if employed.

When Mr. Drummond and Walter came out of the parlor, Joshua was waiting in the next room, and looked up eagerly to see how his father bore the communication. He was disappointed when he saw that Mr. Drummond looked much as usual.

"Conrad has been telling me," said Mr. Drummond, "that his father lost a good deal of money by speculation, and it is doubtful whether he has left any property."

"I am very sorry," said Mrs. Drummond; and Walter saw and appreciated her look of sympathy.

"As he will probably have to work for a living, he has asked for a place in my store," pursued Mr. Drummond, "and I have agreed to take him on trial. Conrad, you may get your hat and come over at once."

Joshua whistled in sheer amazement. The affair had by no means terminated as he anticipated.

CHAPTER X. MR. DRUMMOND'S STORE.

Mr. Drummond's store was of fair size, and contained a considerable and varied stock of dry goods. Not only the people of Stapleton, but a considerable number of persons living outside the town limits, but within a radius of half-a-dozen miles, came there to purchase goods.

Besides Mr. Drummond there was a single salesman, a young man of twenty-two, who wore a cravat of immense size, and ostentatiously displayed in his bosom a mammoth breastpin, with a glass imitation diamond, which, had it been real, would have been equal in value to the entire contents of the store. This young man, whose name was Nichols, received from Mr. Drummond the munificent salary of four hundred dollars per annum. Having a taste for dress, he patronized the village tailor to the extent of his means, and considerably beyond, being at this moment thirty dollars in debt for the suit he wore.

Besides this young man, there had formerly been a younger clerk, receiving a salary of four dollars weekly. He had been dismissed for asking to have his pay raised to five dollars a week, and since then Mr. Drummond had got along with but one salesman. As, however, the business really required more assistance, he was quite willing to employ Walter on board wages, which he estimated would not cost him, at the most, more than two dollars a week.

"Mr. Nichols," said Mr. Drummond, "I have brought you some help. This is Walter Conrad, a distant relative." (Had Walter been rich, he would have been a near relative.) "He knows nothing of the business. You can take him in charge, and give him some idea about prices, and so forth."

"Yes, sir," said the young man, in an important tone. "I'll soon break him in."

Mr. Nichols, who gave up what little mind he had to the subject of clothes, began to inspect Walter's raiment. He had sufficient knowledge to perceive that our hero's suit was of fine fabric, and tastefully made. That being the case, he concluded to pay him some attention.

"I'm glad you've come," he said. "I have to work like a dog. I'm pretty well used up to-day. I was up till two o'clock dancing."

"Were you?"

"Yes. There was a ball over to Crampton. I go to all the balls within ten miles. They can't do without me."

"Can't they?" asked Walter, not knowing what else to say.

"No. You see there isn't much style at these country balls, —I mean among the young men. They don't know how to dress. Now I give my mind to it, and they try to imitate me. I don't trust any tailor entirely. I just tell him what I want, and how I want it. Higgins, the tailor here, has improved a good deal since he began to make clothes for me."

"Indeed!"

"Where do you have your clothes made?"

"In Willoughby. That's where I have always lived till I came here."

"Is there a good tailor there?"

"I think so; but then I am not much of a judge."

Just then a customer came in, and Mr. Nichols was drawn away from his dissertation on dress.

"Just notice how I manage," he said in a low voice.

Accordingly Walter stood by and listened.

"Have you any calicoes that you can recommend?" asked the woman, who appeared to be poor.

"Yes, ma'am, we've got some of the best in the market,—some that will be sure to suit you."

He took from the shelves and displayed a very ugly pattern.

"I don't think I like that," she said. "Haven't you got some with a smaller figure?"

"The large figures are all the rage just now, ma'am. Everybody wears them."

"Is that so?" asked the woman, irresolutely.

"Fact, I assure you."

"How much is it a yard?"

"Fifteen cents only."

"Are you sure it will wash?"

"Certainly."

"I should like to look at something else."

"I'll show you something else, but this is the thing for you."

He brought out a piece still uglier; and finally, after some hesitation, his customer ordered ten yards from the first piece. He measured it with an air, and, folding it up, handed it to the customer, receiving in return a two-dollar bill, which the poor woman sighed as she rendered in, for she had worked hard for it.

"Is there anything more, ma'am?"

"A spool of cotton, No. 100."

When the customer had left the store, Nichols turned complacently to Walter.

"How did you like that calico?" he asked.

"It seemed to me very ugly."

"Wasn't it, though? It's been in the store five years. I didn't know as we should ever get rid of it."

"I thought you said it was all the rage."

"That's all gammon, of course."

"Haven't you got any prettier patterns?"

"Plenty."

"Why didn't you show them?"

"I wanted to get off the old rubbish first. It isn't everybody that would buy it; but she swallowed everything I said."

"She seemed like a poor woman, who couldn't afford to buy a dress very often."

"No, she doesn't come more than twice a year."

"I think you ought to have given her the best bargain you could."

"You don't understand the business, Walter," said Nichols, complacently.

"Mr. Drummond," he said, going up to his employer, "I've just sold ten yards of those old-style calicoes."

"Very good," said Mr. Drummond, approvingly. "Shove them off whenever you get a chance."

"If that is the way they do business, I shan't like it," thought Walter.

"You can fold up those goods on the counter, and put them back on the shelves," said Nichols. "Customers put us to a great deal of trouble that way sometimes. Mrs. Captain Walker was in yesterday afternoon, and I didn't know but I should have to get down all the stock we had before we could suit her."

"Why didn't you pick out something, and tell her it was all the rage?" said Walter, smiling.

"That wouldn't go down with her. She's rich and she's proud. We have to be careful how we manage with such customers as she is. That reminds me that her bundle hasn't gone home yet. I'll get you to carry it up right away."

"I don't know where she lives."

"It's a large, square white house, about a quarter of a mile down the road, at the left hand. You can't miss it."

The bundle was produced, and Walter set off in the direction indicated. He had only gone a few rods when he overtook Joshua, who was sauntering along with a fishing-pole in his hand.

"Where are you going with that big bundle?" asked Joshua.

"To Mrs. Captain Walker's."

"I'll show you where it is. I'm going that way."

Joshua's manner was considerably less deferential than the day before, when he supposed Walter to be rich. Now he looked upon him as his father's hired boy.

"Isn't that bundle heavy?" he asked.

"Yes, rather heavy."

"I wouldn't be seen carrying such a bundle."

"Why not?"

"I feel above it."

"I don't."

"It's different with you—now I mean. My father's worth money, and I suppose you will be poor."

"I don't mean to be poor all my life, but I shall have to work for all the money I am worth."

"It'll take a good while to get rich that way. If your father hadn't lost his money, you could have fine times."

"I don't know about that. I never cared so much about inheriting money."

They were passing the village school-house. Through the open windows floated the strain of a song which the children were singing. This was the verse which the boys heard:—

"It's all very well to depend on a friend,— That is, if you've proved him true; But you'll find it better by far in the end To paddle your own canoe. To 'borrow' is dearer by far than to 'buy,'— A maxim, though old, still true; You never will sigh, if you only will try To paddle your own canoe!"

"That is going to be my motto," said Walter.

"What?"

"'Paddle your own canoe.' I'm going to depend upon myself, and I mean to succeed."

"That's all very well, if you've got to do it; but I expect the old man will leave me twenty-five thousand dollars, and that's a good deal better than paddling my own canoe."

"Suppose your father should fail?"

"There isn't any danger. He'll take good care of his money, I'll warrant that. I wish he wasn't so mighty stingy, for I'd like a little now. But there's Captain Walker's. I'll wait here, while you go and leave the bundle."

Walter performed his errand, and rejoined Joshua, who had seated himself on the fence.

"I'm going a-fishing," said Joshua. "If you didn't have to work you could go with me."

"I must hurry back to the store."

So the two parted company.

"I wish he'd been rich," thought Joshua. "I'd have borrowed some money of him. It won't pay to be polite to him, now it turns out he isn't worth a cent."

Walter went back to the store with a lighter heart than before. There was something in the song he had heard which gave him new strength and hopefulness, and he kept repeating over to himself at intervals, "Paddle your own canoe!"

CHAPTER XI. JOSHUA STIRS UP THE WRONG CUSTOMER.

When Walter went into the house to dinner, the appearance of the table indicated the truth of what Joshua had told him. Since Mr. Drummond had ascertained the pecuniary position of his visitor, he no longer felt it incumbent upon him to keep up appearances. Corned beef and potatoes, and bread without butter, constituted the mid-day meal. This certainly differed considerably from the supper and breakfast of which Walter had partaken.

"Sit right down, Conrad," said Mr. Drummond. "Eat your dinner as fast as you can, and go back to the store."

It did not take Walter long to eat his dinner. Corned beef he had never liked, though now, having no choice, he managed to eat a little.

"If you're through, you needn't wait for me," said Mr. Drummond. "We don't stand on ceremony here. Tell Nichols he may go to his dinner. I'll be right over; so, if there are any customers you can't wait on, ask them to wait."

In the evening Walter found that his carpet-bag had been removed from the spare chamber to a small, uncarpeted back room, furnished with the barest necessaries.

He smiled to himself.

"I shan't be in danger of forgetting my change of circumstances," he said to himself.

He was tired, however, and, though the bed was harder than he had ever before slept on, he managed to sleep soundly. He was waked up early by Mr. Drummond.

"Hurry up, Conrad!" said that gentleman, unceremoniously. "I want you to be up within fifteen minutes to open the store."

Walter jumped out of bed and hurriedly dressed. His position was so new that he did not at first realize it. When he did reflect that he was working for his board in a country store, he hardly knew whether to feel glad or sorry. He had begun to earn his living, and this was satisfactory; but he was working for a man whom he could neither like nor respect, and his pay was very poor of its kind. That was not so agreeable.

Walter was not a glutton, nor inordinately fond of good living, but he had the appetite of a healthy boy, and when he entered the room where breakfast was spread (this was after he had been in the store an hour), he did wish that there had been something on the table besides the remains of the corned beef and a plate of bread and butter.

"Do you take sugar and milk in your tea, Walter?" asked Mrs. Drummond.

"If you please."

"I don't take either," remarked Mr. Drummond. "It's only a habit, and an expensive one. If you'd try going without for a week, you would cure yourself of the habit."

"How intolerably mean he is!" thought Walter, for he understood very well that the only consideration in Mr. Drummond's mind was the expense.

"I don't think I shall ever learn to go without milk and sugar," said Walter, quietly, not feeling disposed to humor his employer in this little meanness.

"There isn't anything fit to eat on the table," grumbled Joshua, looking about him discontentedly.

"You are always complaining," said his father, sharply. "If you earned your breakfast, you wouldn't be so particular."

"Why can't you have beefsteak once in a while, instead of corned beef? I'm sick to death of corned beef."

"We shall have some beefsteak on Sunday morning, and not till then. I don't mean to pamper your appetite."

"That's so!" said Joshua. "Not much danger of that."

"If you are not satisfied, you can go without."

"I will, then," said Joshua, rising from the table.

He knew very well that as soon as his father had gone to

the store he could get something better from his mother.

It had been a considerable disappointment to Joshua to find that Walter was poor instead of rich, for he had proposed to make as free use of Walter's purse as the latter would permit. Even now it occurred to him that Walter might have a supply of ready money, a part of which he might borrow. He accordingly took an opportunity during the day to sound our hero on this subject.

"Walter, have you a couple of dollars about you to lend me for a day or two?" he asked, in a tone of assumed carelessness.

"Yes, I have that amount of money, but I am afraid I must decline lending."

"Why shouldn't you lend me? It's only for a day or two."

But Walter knew very well Joshua's small allowance, and that he would not be able to return a loan of that amount, even if he were desirous of so doing, and he judged Joshua so well that he doubted whether he would have any such desire.

"You know my circumstances, Joshua," he said, "and that I am in no position to lend anybody money."

"Two dollars isn't much. You said you had it."

"Yes, I have it; but I must take care of what little I have. I am working for my board, as you know, and have got to provide for all my other expenses myself; therefore I shall need all my money."

"You talk as if I wanted you to *give* me the money. I only asked you to lend it."

"That's about the same thing," thought Walter; but he only said, "Why don't you ask your father for the money?"

"Because he wouldn't give it to me. He's as mean as dirt."

"Then where would you get the money to repay me in case I lent it to you?"

"You're just as mean as he is," exclaimed Joshua, angrily, not caring to answer this question. "A mighty fuss you make about lending a fellow a couple of dollars!"

"It makes no particular difference to me whether you think me mean or not," said Walter. "I have got to be richer than I am now before I lend money."

Joshua stalked away in a fret, angry that Walter would not permit himself to be swindled. From that time he cherished a dislike to our hero, and this he showed by various little slights and annoyances, of which Walter took little notice. He thoroughly despised Joshua for his meanness and selfishness, and it mattered very little to him what such a boy thought of him.

This forbearance Joshua utterly misinterpreted. He decided that Walter was deficient in courage and spirit, and it encouraged him to persevere in his system of petty annoyances until they might almost be called bullying. Though Walter kept quiet under these provocations, there was often a warning flash of the eye which showed that it would not be safe to go too far. But this Joshua did not notice, and persisted.

"Joshua," said his mother one day, "I really think you don't treat Walter right. You are not polite to him."

"Why should I be? What is he but a beggar?"

"He is not that, for he works for his living."

"At any rate he's a mean fellow, and I shall treat him as I please."

But one day matters came to a climax.

One afternoon there were a few young fellows standing on the piazza in front of Mr. Drummond's store. Joshua was one of them, and there being no customers to wait upon, Walter also had joined the company. They were discussing plans for a picnic to be held in the woods on the next Saturday afternoon. It was to be quite a general affair.

"You will come, Walter, won't you?" asked one of the number.

"No," said Joshua; "he can't come."

"I didn't authorize you to speak for me," said Walter,

quietly.

"You didn't authorize me to speak for you?" repeated Joshua, in a mocking tone. "Big words for a beggar!"

"What do you mean by calling me a beggar?" demanded Walter, quietly, but with rising color.

"I don't choose to give you any explanation," said Joshua, scornfully. "You're only my father's hired boy, working for your board."

"That may be true, but I am not a beggar, and I advise you not to call me one again."

Walter's tone was still quiet, and Joshua wholly misunderstood him; otherwise, being a coward at heart, he would have desisted.

"I'll say it as often as I please," he repeated. "You're a beggar, and if we hadn't taken pity on you, you'd have had to go to the poor-house."

Walter was not quarrelsome; but this last insult, in presence of half-a-dozen boys between his own age and Joshua's, roused him.

"Joshua Drummond," he said, "you've insulted me long enough, and I've stood it, for I didn't want to quarrel; but I will stand it no longer."

He walked up to Joshua, and struck him in the face, not a hard blow, but still a blow.

Joshua turned white with passion, and advanced upon our hero furiously, with the intention of giving him, as he expressed it, the worst whipping he ever had.

Walter parried his blow, and put in another, this time sharp and stinging. Joshua was an inch or two taller, but Walter was more than a match for him. Joshua threw out his arms, delivering his blows at random, and most of them failed of effect. Indeed, he was so blinded with rage, that Walter, who kept cool, had from this cause alone a great advantage over him. Joshua at length seized him, and he was compelled to throw him down. As Joshua lay prostrate, with Walter's knee upon his breast, Mr. Drummond, who had gone over to his own house, appeared upon the scene.

"What's all this?" he demanded in mingled surprise and anger. "Conrad, what means this outrageous conduct?"

Walter rose, and, turning to his employer, said, manfully, "Joshua insulted me, sir, and I have punished him. That's all!"

CHAPTER XII. AFTER THE BATTLE.

Without waiting to hear Mr. Drummond's reply to his explanation, Walter re-entered the store. He had no disposition to discuss the subject in presence of the boys who were standing on the piazza.

Mr. Drummond followed him into the store, and Joshua accompanied him. He was terribly angry with Walter, and determined to get revenged upon him through his father.

"Are you going to let that beggar pitch into me like that?" he demanded. "He wouldn't have got me down, only he took me at disadvantage."

"Conrad," said Mr. Drummond, "I demand an explanation of your conduct. I come from my house, and find you fighting like a street rowdy, instead of attending to your duties in the store."

"I have already given you an explanation, Mr. Drummond," said Walter, firmly. "Joshua chose to insult me before all the boys, and I don't allow myself to be insulted if I can help it. As to being out of the store, there was no customer to wait upon, and I went to the door for a breath of fresh air. I have never been accustomed to such confinement before."

"You say Joshua insulted you. How did he insult you?"

"I was asked if I would go to the picnic on Saturday afternoon. He didn't wait for me to answer, but said at once that I couldn't come."

"Was that all?"

"On my objecting to his answering for me, he charged me with being a beggar, and said that but for you I would have been obliged to go to the poor-house. If this had been the first time he had annoyed me, I might have passed it over, but it is far from being the first; so I knocked him down."

Mr. Drummond was by no means a partisan of Walter, but in the month that our hero had been in his employ he had found him a very efficient clerk. Whatever Walter undertook to do he did well, and he had mastered the details of the retail dry-goods trade in a remarkably short time, so that his services were already nearly as valuable as those of young Nichols, who received eight dollars a week. Therefore Mr. Drummond was disposed to smooth over matters, for the sake of retaining the services which he obtained so cheap. He resolved, therefore, to temporize.

"You are both of you wrong," he said. "Joshua, you should not have called Conrad a beggar, for he earns his living. You, Conrad, should not have been so violent. You should have told me, and I would have spoken to Joshua."

"Excuse me, Mr. Drummond, but I don't like tale-bearing. I did the only thing I could."

"Ahem!" said Mr. Drummond, "you were too violent. I would suggest that you should each beg the other's pardon, shake hands, and have done with it."

"Catch me begging pardon of my father's hired boy!" exclaimed Joshua scornfully. "I haven't got quite so low as that."

"As for me," said Walter, "if I thought I had been in the wrong, I would beg Joshua's pardon without any hesitation. I am not too proud for that, but I think I acted right under the circumstances, and therefore I cannot do it. As for being a hired boy, I admit that such is my position, and I don't see anything to be ashamed of in it."

"You are right there," said Mr. Drummond; for this assertion chimed in with his own views and wishes. "Well, it seems to me you are about even, and you may as well drop the quarrel here."

"I am ready to do so," said Walter, promptly. "If Joshua treats me well, I will treat him well."

"You're mighty accommodating," sneered Joshua. "You seem to think you're on an equality with me."

"I am willing to treat you as an equal," answered Walter, purposely misinterpreting Joshua's remark.

"Oh, you are, are you?" retorted Joshua, with a vicious snap of the eyes. "Do you think you, a hired boy, are equal to me, who am a gentleman?"

"I am glad to hear that you consider yourself a gentleman, and hope you will take care to act like one."

"I'll give you the worst licking you ever had!" exclaimed Joshua, clenching his fists furiously.

"If it isn't any worse than you gave me just now, I can stand it," said Walter.

He was a little angry, also, and this prompted him to speak thus.

Joshua was maddened by this remark, and might have renewed the battle if his father had not imperatively ordered him to leave the store.

"Conrad," said Mr. Drummond, "you have behaved badly. I did not think you were so quarrelsome."

"I don't think I am, sir; but I cannot stand Joshua's treatment."

"Will you promise not to quarrel with him again?"

"That depends on whether he provokes me."

"Of course I can't have you fighting with my son."

"I don't care about doing it. If I find he won't let me alone, I have made up my mind what to do."

"What?"

"I will leave the store, and go back to Willoughby; then I will decide what to do. I know that I have got to earn my own living, but I would rather earn it somewhere where I can be at peace."

"Humph!" said Mr. Drummond, who did not fancy this determination; "don't be too hasty. I will speak to Joshua, and see that he doesn't annoy you again."

With this assurance Walter felt satisfied. He felt that he had won the victory and maintained his self-respect. There was one thing more he desired, and that was to go to the picnic. He would not have urged the request, but that he was well aware that Joshua would report that he was kept at home by his desire.

"It won't be very convenient for you to be away Saturday afternoon," said Mr. Drummond, who was principled against allowing clerks any privileges. "You know we have more trade than usual on Saturday afternoon."

"I don't think we shall have next Saturday," said Walter; "everybody will be gone to the picnic."

"If you insist upon going," said Mr. Drummond, reluctantly, "I must try to let you go."

Walter felt no scruples about insisting. He knew that he earned his limited pay twice over, and that his absence would do his employer no harm. He answered, therefore, "Thank you, sir; I will be home at six o'clock, so as to be in the store all Saturday evening."

Meanwhile Joshua went home in a very unhappy frame of mind. He had not succeeded in humiliating Walter as he intended, but had an unpleasant feeling that Walter had got the better of him. He was very angry with his father for not taking his part, and was not slow in making his feelings known to his mother.

"What's the matter, Joshua?" asked Mrs. Drummond, observing the scowl upon his face.

"Matter enough! That beggar has been insulting me."

"What beggar? I haven't seen any beggar about," answered Mrs. Drummond.

"You know who I mean,—that upstart, Conrad."

"What's he been doing? I'm sure he's a very gentlemanly young man."

"Oh, yes, that's just the way. You take his part against your own son," said Joshua, bitterly.

"What's he been doing? You haven't told me."

"He pitched into me, and tried to knock me over."

"What for? I am surprised to hear it, he seems so polite and well-bred."

"Nothing at all. He sprung at me like a tiger, and all for nothing. He took me by surprise, so at first he got the advantage; but I soon gave him as good as he sent."

"I am really sorry to hear this," said Mrs. Drummond, distressed. "Are you sure you didn't say something to provoke him?"

"I only said, when he was invited to go to the picnic Saturday afternoon, that he wouldn't be able to leave the store."

"I am afraid you said it in such a way as to offend him."

"Seems to me you think a good sight more of him than of me in the matter," grumbled Joshua. "That's just the way with father. He wanted us both to beg each other's pardon. Catch me begging pardon of a beggarly hired boy!"

"He isn't any worse because your father hires him, Joshua."

"Oh, yes, of course you stand up for him," said Joshua, sneering.

"Now, Joshua, you know I always take your part when you are right."

So Joshua continued to scold, and Mrs. Drummond to soothe him, until she found a more effectual way, by placing at his disposal half an apple-pie which was in the cupboard. In the evening she told Walter that she was sorry there had been any difficulty between him and Joshua.

"So am I," said Walter, frankly, for he was grateful for her gentle kindness. "I am sorry, if only for your sake, Mrs. Drummond."

"I know he's provoking; but he don't mean what he says, Mr. Conrad."

"I'll try to keep on good terms with him, Mrs. Drummond," said Walter, earnestly, "if only in return for his mother's kindness."

"I am sure Joshua was hasty, and misjudged Walter," said the mother to herself, trying to find an excuse for her son.

CHAPTER XIII. THE ARROW AND THE PIONEER.

After this Joshua was more careful about annoying Walter. Though he was older, and a little taller than our hero, he had found to his cost that he was not a match for him in strength. He had also made the unwelcome discovery that Walter did not intend to be imposed upon. So, though he ventured to sneer at times, he thought it best to stop short of open insult. There was also another motive which influenced him. His father forbade him in tones more decided than usual to interfere with Walter, whose services he was anxious to retain in the store. Mr. Drummond also had another reason for this command. He thought that Walter might be mistaken as to the state of his father's affairs, and that a few thousand dollars might be rescued by his executor from the ruin. In that case, there would be a chance of his obtaining control of Walter's property during his minority.

The picnic came off on Saturday afternoon. The weather, which often throws a wet blanket upon the festivities of such occasions, was highly propitious, and several hundred persons, young and middle-aged, turned out *en masse*. The place selected for the picnic was a field of several acres, bordering upon a pond. This had been fitted up by the proprietor with swings, and a roofed building without sides, under which were placed rough board tables for the reception of provisions. A number of oak trees with their broad branches furnished shelter.

Besides these arrangements for enjoyment, there were two boats confined by iron chains, which were thrown around trees near the brink of the water.

After enjoying the swing for a time, there was a proposition to go out in the boats.

The boats could comfortably accommodate eight persons each. This number had been obtained, when Joshua came up.

"I'm going," he said unceremoniously.

"You will have to wait till next time," said Ralph Morse. "We've got the full number."

"No, I'm going this time," said Joshua, rudely.

"I don't believe there's room. We have eight already."

"There's room for nine. If there isn't you can wait till next time yourself. Besides, you want me to steer."

"Do you know how to steer?"

"Of course I do," said Joshua, boastfully.

"I guess we can make room," said Mary Meyer, who was always in favor of peaceful measures.

Joshua clambered in, and took his place as steersman.

The other boat had already set off, and, as it happened, under the guidance of Walter Conrad, who had long been accustomed to managing a boat, having had one of his own at home.

"They've got a great steerer on the other boat," said Joshua, sneering.

"It's your cousin, isn't it? Doesn't he know how to steer?"

"About as well as an old cat. He thinks he does, though."

Attention was thus directed to the other boat, which was making easy progress through the water.

"I don't see but he manages well enough," said Rudolph, after watching it for a moment.

"Oh, it's easy enough steering here. Wait till we get out a little way."

"Where are you steering, Joshua?" asked Ralph, suddenly, for the boat nearly half turned round. The fact was that Joshua himself knew very little about steering. In speaking of Walter's want of skill, he had precisely described himself.

"I understand what I'm about," answered Joshua, suddenly reversing the direction, and overdoing the matter, so as to turn the boat half way round the other way.

"I hope you do," said Ralph, "but it don't look much like it."

"I was looking at the other boat," Joshua condescended to explain, "and the rudder slipped."

Walter's boat kept the lead. His perfect steering made the task easier for the rowers, who got the full advantage of their efforts. Joshua, however, by his uncertain steering, hindered the progress of his boat.

"Can't we beat the other boat?" asked Joseph Wheeler, who was rowing. "I can row as well as either of those fellows."

"So can I," said Tom Barry; "let's try."

The boats were about five lengths apart, the rowers in the foremost boat not having worked very hard, when Tom and Joe began to exert themselves. Their intention was soon manifest, and the spirit of rivalry was excited.

"Do your best, boys!" said Walter. "They're trying to catch us. Don't let them do it."

The rowers of the two boats were about evenly matched. If anything, however, Tom and Joe were superior, and, other things being equal, would sooner or later have won the race. But Joshua, by his original style of steering, which became under the influence of excitement even more unreliable, caused them to lose perceptibly.

"Can't you steer straight by accident, Joshua?" asked Tom, in a tone of vexation.

"I know more about steering than you do, Tom Barry," growled Joshua, getting red in the face, for he could not help seeing that he was not appearing to advantage.

"Show it, then, if you do," was the reply. "If we had your cousin to steer us, we could soon get ahead."

This was very mortifying to Joshua. He did not care to be outdone by any one, but to be outdone by Walter was particularly disagreeable.

"It isn't the steering, it's the rowing," he said. "You don't row even."

"Won't you try it, then," said Joe, "and show us what you can do?"

"No, I'd rather steer."

Joshua considered that the steersman's place was the place of honor, and he was not disposed to yield it.

Meanwhile Walter, from his place in the first boat, watched the efforts of his rivals. He was determined to keep the lead which he had secured, and had little fear of losing it.

"Give way, boys!" he cried; "we'll distance them, never fear!"

Every moment increased the distance between the two boats, to the great satisfaction of those on board the "Arrow," for that was the name of the head boat.

Just at the north-western corner of the pond there was an inlet of considerable length, but narrow. Here the water was shallower than in the remainder of the pond.

"Shall we go in there?" asked Walter.

"Yes, yes," said his fellow-passengers.

Accordingly he steered in, and shortly afterwards the "Pioneer," Joshua's boat, also entered. At this time the distance between the two boats was quite two hundred feet.

The "Arrow" pursued her way steadily to the head of the inlet, a distance of nearly a quarter of a mile; and then making a graceful turn, started on her homeward trip. The width of the inlet here was very much contracted. After making the turn the "Arrow" met the "Pioneer" after a little distance. There was abundant room for the boats to pass each other, if they had been properly managed. There was no fault in Walter's steering, but, by an awkward blunder of Joshua's, the "Pioneer" veered in her course so that the "Arrow" struck her, to use a nautical term, amidships. As she was being impelled rapidly at the time, the shock was considerable, and the fright still greater. The girls jumped to their feet screaming, and Joshua himself turned pale with fright, but recovered himself sufficiently to call out angrily, "What made you run into us, you fool?"

"It's your own fault, Joshua," said Tom Barry, angrily. "You're the most stupid steerer I ever saw. What made you turn the boat?"

"It's his fault," said Joshua, doggedly.

"Let somebody else steer," said Joe Wheeler. "A baby could steer better than he."

So a younger boy was put in Joshua's place, much to his mortification, and he was degraded, as he considered it, to the rank of a passenger.

"I'm going ashore," he said sourly. "Let me out up here."

"All right!" said Tom Barry. "I guess we can get along without you. Here, you fellows on the "Arrow," just wait a minute, till we've landed Joshua, and we'll race you back."

True to his determination, Joshua jumped off at the head of the inlet, and the "Pioneer" was turned by her new pilot.

The "Arrow" and the "Pioneer" took their places side by side, and the race commenced. The boats were similar, and thus neither had the advantage on this score. But the rowers on the "Pioneer" were on the whole stronger and more skilful than those on the "Arrow." On the other hand, Walter steered perfectly, while Joshua's successor, though he made no bad blunder, was a novice.

The result was that the race was a clear one. Finally the "Arrow" came in a length ahead, and Walter felt with quiet satisfaction that the victory had been gained by his efforts.

He thought once more of the song he had heard, and hoped that he would be as successful through life in paddling his own canoe.

Joshua went home sulky, and was not seen again on the picnic grounds.

CHAPTER XIV. A BRILLIANT SCHEME.

One morning, a few days later, Joshua was walking moodily up the village road with his hands in his pockets. He was reflecting, in a spirit of great discontent, on the hardships of his situation.

"Here am I," he said to himself, "eighteen years old, and father treats me like a boy of ten. I'm most a man, and all he gives me for pocket-money is twenty-five cents a week. There's Dick Storrs, whose father isn't a quarter as rich as mine, gets a dollar a week. He's only sixteen, too."

One important difference between himself and Dick Storrs did not occur to Joshua. Dick worked in a shoe-shop, and it was out of his own wages that his father allowed him a dollar a week. Joshua earned nothing at all.

"It's mean!" reflected Joshua. "There aint a boy of my age in Stapleton that's so meanly treated, and yet my father's the richest man in town. I wish I knew what to do to get a little money."

At this moment he saw Sam Crawford approaching him. Sam was perhaps a year younger than Joshua. He had formerly lived in the village, but was now in a situation in New York, and was only in Stapleton for a few days.

"How are you, Joshua?" said Sam.

"Well enough," said Joshua. "Where are you going?"

"I'm going round to the ice-cream saloon. Won't you come with me?"

"Yes, if you'll treat. I haven't got any money."

"You ought to have. The old man's got plenty."

"That's so. But he's getting meaner every day. What do you think he allows me for spending money?"

"I don't know. A dollar a week?"

"A dollar! I should think myself lucky if I got anywhere near that. What do you say to twenty-five cents?"

"You don't mean to say that's all he gives you?"

"Yes, I do."

"Why, I can't get along on ten times that. Why don't you ask for more?"

"I have, fifty times; but that's all the good it does."

"If my father treated me like that, I'd cut his acquaintance."

"I don't know as that would do me any good," said Joshua, rather sensibly. "I wish I knew of any way of getting some money."

"You might hire out to saw wood for the neighbors," said Sam.

"I haven't got so low as that," said Joshua, haughtily.

"Of course I meant that in joke; but you might get a place, and earn some money."

This suggestion, however, did not suit Joshua, for it carried with it the idea of work, and he was as lazy as he was selfish; which is saying as much as can well be said on that point.

"The old man ought to give me enough to spend, without work," he said. "He don't spend more than a third of his income."

"He's saving it up for you."

"I'm not likely to get it for a good many years," said Joshua, who actually seemed to be angry with his father for living so long. However, though it is doubtful whether Joshua would have been a dutiful or affectionate son under any circumstances, it must be admitted that Mr. Drummond had done very little to inspire filial affection.

"Look here!" said Sam, suddenly, "I have an idea. Did you ever buy a lottery ticket?"

"No," answered Joshua.

"There's a fellow I know in New York that drew a prize of a thousand dollars, and how much do you think he paid for a ticket?"

"I don't know."

"Five dollars. How's that for high?"

"How long ago is that?" asked Joshua, becoming interested.

"Only two months ago."

"Do you know him?"

"Yes, I know him as well as I know you. He is clerk in a store just opposite ours. When he got the money he gave half a dozen of us a big dinner at Delmonico's. We had a jolly time."

"A thousand dollars for five!" repeated Joshua. "He was awfully lucky. What lottery was it?"

"It was one of the Delaware lotteries."

"Do you know the name of it?"

"No, but I'll tell you what I'll do. The fellow I was speaking of gets lottery papers regularly. I'll ask him for one, and send it to you as soon as I get back to the city."

"I wish you would," said Joshua. "Wouldn't it be splendid if I could draw a prize of a thousand dollars?"

"I'll bet it would. It would make you independent of the old man. You wouldn't care much for his twenty-five cents a week then?"

"No, I'd tell him he might keep it till he got rich enough to afford me more."

"He'd open his eyes a little at that, I reckon."

"I guess he would. When are you going back to the city?"

"The last of this month. My time will be up then."

"You won't forget to send me the paper?"

"No, I'll remember it. Come in and have an ice-cream. You can return the compliment when you've drawn a prize."

"All right! Is a thousand dollars the highest prize?"

"No, there are some of two, three, and five thousand. Then there are five-hundred-dollar prizes, and so along to five dollars. Five hundred wouldn't be so bad, eh?"

"No, I should feel satisfied with that. I would come up to New York, and spend a week."

"If you do, just step in upon me, and I'll show you round. I know the ropes."

"I wish I could," said Joshua, enviously. "This is an awfully stupid place. I tried to get leave to go to the city last fall, but the old man wouldn't let me. He wasn't willing to spend the money."

I hope none of my readers will so admire the character of Joshua Drummond as to imitate him in the disrespectful manner in which he speaks of his father. Yet I am aware that many boys and young men, who are not without respect and affection for their parents, have fallen into the very discreditable way of referring to them as "the old man" or "the old woman." They may be sure that such a habit will prejudice against them all persons of right feeling.

Joshua and Sam went into the ice-cream saloon, which was kept, during the summer only, in a small candy store, by a maiden lady who eked out a scanty income by such limited patronage as the village could afford. Joshua plied his companion with further questions, to all of which he readily replied, though it is doubtful whether all the answers were quite correct. But Sam, having been in the city a few months, wished to be thought to have a very extensive acquaintance with it, and was unwilling to admit ignorance on any point.

Early the next week Sam returned to his duties in the city, and Joshua awaited impatiently the promised lottery papers.

Sam did not forget his promise. On the third day after his departure a paper came to the village post-office, directed.

Joshua Drummond, Esq., Stapleton

This was promptly taken from the office by Joshua, who had called on an average twice a day for this very paper. It proved to be printed on yellow paper, and fairly bristled with figures, indicating the large sums which were weekly distributed all over the country by the benevolent managers of the lottery. Here was a scheme in which the principal prize was but a thousand dollars. However, the tickets were but a dollar each, and a thousand dollars for one was certainly a handsome return for a small outlay. There were others, however, in which the principal prize was five thousand dollars, and the tickets were, in due proportion, five dollars each.

Joshua went off to a somewhat secluded place, for he did not wish to be interrupted, and eagerly read the paper through from beginning to end. Certainly the representations made were of a very seductive character. One might suppose, from reading the paragraphs sandwiching the several schemes, that the chances were strongly in favor of every holder of a ticket drawing a prize, though a little calculation would have shown that the chances of drawing even the smallest prize were scarcely more than one in a hundred. Here, for instance, is one of the paragraphs:—

"A mechanic in a country town in New York State met with an accident which confined him to his home for three months. He had a large family of children, and had never been able to lay up any money. The consequence was, that the family was reduced to great distress, and he saw no resource except to try to borrow a little money, which would create a debt that he might be years in paying off. But fortunately, only a week before the accident, his wife had seen one of our advertisements. She had five dollars by her, which she had intended to appropriate to the purchase of a new dress. Instead of doing this, a happy impulse led her to send for one of our tickets. She concealed this from her husband, however, thinking that he would blame her. What was her joy, when they were reduced to their last dollar, to receive from us intelligence that she had drawn a prize of two thousand dollars! The joy of the poor family can better be imagined than described. They were enabled at once to purchase the house in which they lived, and thus to lay the foundation of permanent prosperity. Thus, as in numberless other cases, have we been the means of bringing joy to lucky households."

Now, this story was probably manufactured out of whole cloth. At any rate, even if true, for every such fortunate household there were a hundred to which the lottery had carried disappointment and privation. But of course the lottery managers could not be expected to allude to these, nor did Joshua, as he greedily read such paragraphs, consider them. On the contrary, his imagination and cupidity were both excited, and he was foolish enough to suppose that his chances of success in case he invested would be very good indeed.

CHAPTER XV. WAYS AND MEANS.

Having decided to purchase a lottery ticket, the important question suggested itself, "Where was he to obtain the necessary five dollars?"

To most boys or young men of eighteen this would not have been a difficult question to solve. But to Joshua it was a perplexing problem. If he saved his entire weekly allowance, it would take him twenty weeks to obtain the needed sum. This delay was not to be thought of. Was there any pretext on which he could ask his father for five dollars? He could think of none that would be likely to succeed. Had he been trusted with the purchase of his own clothes, he might have asked for a new coat and misapplied the money; but Mr. Drummond took care to order Joshua's clothes himself from the village tailor, and never did so without grumbling at the expense he was obliged to incur. Indeed, Joshua was not able to boast much of his clothes, for his father was not disposed to encourage extravagance in dress.

"Perhaps mother may have the money," thought Joshua. "If she has, I'll get it out of her."

He resolved at once to find out whether any help was to be obtained from this quarter, and with this object turned his steps at once homeward.

Mrs. Drummond was engaged in the homely employment of darning stockings when Joshua entered the house.

"You're home early, Joshua," she remarked, looking up.

"Yes, mother. Have you got anything good to eat?"

"I baked a small pie for you in a saucer. I thought that was the best way. The other evening your father noticed that a piece was gone from the half pie that was taken from the supper-table."

"How awful mean he is!"

"You shouldn't say that of your father, Joshua."

"It's true, mother, and you know it. He's the meanest man in town."

"I don't like to hear you talk in that way, Joshua. Don't forget that he is your father."

"I wish he'd treat me like a father, then. I leave it to you, mother, if twenty-five cents a week isn't a miserable allowance for a fellow of my age."

"It is rather small," said Mrs. Drummond, cautiously.

"Small! I should think it was. It's just about right for a boy of ten. That's just the way he treats me."

"Perhaps, if you would speak to your father about it, Joshua—"

"I have spoken to him, and that's all the good it does. He blows me up for my extravagance. Extravagance on twenty-five cents a week!"

"I'll speak to him myself, Joshua," said his mother;—a heroic resolve, for she knew that the request would bring anger upon herself.

"He won't mind your talk any more than mine. But I'll tell you what you can do to oblige me, mother."

"Well, Joshua?"

"I know of a way to make considerable money, and all I need to go into it is five dollars. If you'll lend me that, I'll pay it back to you as soon as I can. I think it won't be more than a fortnight."

"What is the plan you are thinking of, Joshua?"

But upon this subject Joshua thought it best to preserve a discreet silence. He knew that the lottery scheme would not impress his mother favorably, and that she would not lend the money for any such purpose. He was aware in what light lotteries are generally regarded. Still his imagination had been inflamed by the stories he had read of other persons' luck, and he had succeeded in convincing himself that his own chance would be very good. Thus he referred to it, in speaking to his mother, as if he were sure of obtaining a large amount for his investment.

"I can't tell you just at present, mother," he said; "the fact is, somebody else is concerned in it, and I am not allowed to tell."

"I hope, Joshua, you have not allowed yourself to be imposed upon. You know you are not used to business."

"I know what I'm about, mother. I'm not a baby. All I want is the money. Can you lend me five dollars?"

"I wish I could; but you know your father doesn't allow me much money. I get my dress patterns and most of what I want out of the store, so I don't need it."

"You have to buy things for the house,—groceries, and so on."

"We have a bill at the grocery store. Your father pays it quarterly; so no money passes through my hands for that purpose."

"Then you haven't got the money, mother," said Joshua, disappointed.

"I haven't had as much as five dollars in my possession at one time for years," answered his mother.

It was true that Mr. Drummond kept his wife uncommonly close. She was allowed to obtain a limited amount of goods from the store for her own wardrobe, but apart from that her husband appeared to think she had no need of money. More than once she wished she could have a little money at her control to answer occasional calls for charity. But on one occasion, having been indiscreet enough to give twenty-five cents and a good meal to a woman, sick and poor, who crawled to her door and asked for help, Mr. Drummond indulged in such a display of ill-humor at her foolish extravagance, as he called it, that she was forced afterwards to deny her generous impulses, or give in the most secret manner, pledging the recipient to silence.

"I'm sorry I can't oblige you, Joshua," said his mother. "Will you have the pie?"

"Yes," said Joshua, sullenly, for he was at a loss where next to apply, and felt that his scheme of sudden riches was blighted at its inception. Notwithstanding his disappointment, however, he was able to dispose of the pie. After consuming it, he went out of doors, to reflect upon other ways of raising the necessary money.

There was his cousin Walter; he was quite sure that he had the money, but quite as sure that he would not lend it. Besides, he would have hesitated to apply, on account of the dislike he had come to entertain for our hero. This dislike had been increased by the result of the boat race between the "Pioneer" and the "Arrow." He had occasion to know that the defeat of the former boat was generally ascribed to his own imperfect steering, and he also knew that Walter had obtained considerable credit for his own performance in the same line. Now Joshua knew in his own heart that he could not steer, but he wanted the reputation of steering well, and it was very irksome to him to have to play second fiddle to Walter. He had indicated his dislike ever since by refusing to notice or speak to Walter, except in so far as it was absolutely necessary. Of course Walter noticed this want of cordiality, and was in a measure sorry for it; still he had become pretty thoroughly acquainted with Joshua's character by this time, and this knowledge led him to feel that the loss of his friendship was not a very serious one. He had made some other acquaintances, in the village, with boys of his own age, in whose society he found considerable more pleasure than he was ever likely to do in Joshua's.

"He can go his way, and I'll go mine," he said to himself. "I'll paddle my own canoe, and he may paddle his. Perhaps he will succeed better in that than in steering," he thought with a smile.

Help from Walter, therefore, was not to be expected. Was there any one else to help him?

Joshua thought doubtfully of his father's clerk, young Nichols, who has already been introduced to the reader. He did not think there was much prospect of obtaining a loan from

Nichols; still there might be. At any rate there seemed no other resource, and he made up his mind to sound him.

He stepped into the store one day when Walter was absent on an errand, and his father was out also.

"Good-morning, Joshua," said the salesman. "What's up this morning?"

"Nothing that I know of."

"You have an easy time. Nothing to do but to lounge about all day. You aint cooped up in a store fourteen hours a day."

"That's so; but I suppose I'll have to begin some time."

"Oh, you're all right. Your father's getting richer every year."

"Yes, I suppose he is; but that doesn't give me ready money now. The fact is, I'm hard up for five dollars. Can't you lend it to me for a week? I'll give it back in a week, or ten days at any rate."

"You couldn't come to a worse place for money," said Nichols, laughing. "The fact is, I'm hard up myself, and always am. Old Jones, the tailor, is dunning me for this very suit I have on. Fact is, my salary is so small, I have the hardest kind of work to get along."

"Then you can't lend me the money? It's for only a week I want it."

"I've got less than a dollar in my pocket, and I'm owing about fifty dollars to the tailor and shoemaker. Perhaps Walter can lend you the money."

"I shan't ask him," said Joshua, shortly. "I'll go without first."

"Don't you like him?"

"No, I don't. He's a mean fellow."

Nichols was privately of the opinion that the term described Joshua himself much more aptly, but did not express his opinion.

CHAPTER XVI. JOSHUA TRIES KEEPING STORE.

The more Joshua thought it over, the more convinced he was that a large sum of money was likely to come to him through the lottery, if he could only manage to raise money enough to buy a ticket. But the problem of how to get the necessary five dollars he was as far as ever from solving.

While in this state of mind he happened one day to be in the store at noon, and alone. Nichols, the head clerk, wished to go to dinner, and was only waiting for Walter to get back from an errand.

"I wish Walter would hurry up," he grumbled. "My dinner will get cold."

"I'll take your place till he gets back, Mr. Nichols," said Joshua, with extraordinary kindness for him.

"Much obliged, Joshua," said the salesman. "I'll do as much for you another time. I don't think you'll have long to wait."

"You'd better hurry off," said Joshua. "I'd just as lief wait as not."

"I never knew him so accommodating before," thought Nichols, with a feeling of surprise.

He seized his hat and hurried away.

No sooner had he gone than Joshua, after following him to the door, and looking carefully up and down the street, walked behind the counter with a hasty step, and opened the money-drawer.

There was a small pile of bills in one compartment, and in the other a collection of currency. He took the bills into his hand, and looked over them. His hands trembled a little, for he contemplated a dishonest act. Unable to obtain the money in any other way, he meant to borrow (that was what he called it) five dollars from the money-drawer, and expend it in a lottery ticket.

Singling out a five-dollar bill from the pile, he thrust it into his vest-pocket. He had scarcely done so when he was startled by hearing the door open. He made a guilty jump, but perceived, to his relief, that it was a woman not living in the village, but probably in some adjoining town.

"What can I show you, ma'am?" he asked, in a flurried manner, for he could not help thinking of what he had in his vest-pocket.

"I should like to look at some of your shawls," said the woman.

Joshua knew very little about his father's stock. He did know, however, where the shawls were kept, and going to that portion of the shelves, pulled down half a dozen and showed them to his customer.

"Are they all wool?" she asked, critically examining one of them.

"Yes," answered Joshua, confidently, though he had not the slightest knowledge on the subject.

"What is the price of this one?" asked the customer, indicating the one she had in her hand.

"Five dollars," answered Joshua, with some hesitation. He knew nothing of the price, but guessed that this would be about right.

"And you say it is all wool?"

"Certainly, ma'am."

"I guess I'll take it. Will you wrap it up for me?"

This Joshua did awkwardly enough, and the customer departed, much pleased with her bargain, as she had a right to be, for the real price of the shawl was nine dollars, but, thanks to Joshua's ignorance, she had been able to save four.

Joshua looked at the five-dollar bill he had just received, and a new idea occurred to him. He replaced in the drawer the bill he had originally taken from it, and substituted that just received.

"I won't say anything about having sold a shawl," he said,

"and father'll never know that one has been sold. At any rate, not till I get money enough to replace the bill I have taken."

Just then a little girl came in and inquired for a spool of cotton.

Joshua found the spools, and let her select one.

"How much is it?" asked the young customer.

"Ten cents."

"Mother told me it wouldn't be but six."

"Very well, if that is all you expect to pay, you shall have it for that."

"Thank you, sir;" and the little girl departed with her purchase.

Joshua now hurriedly folded up the shawls and replaced them on the shelves. He had just finished the task when Walter entered.

"Are you tending store?" he said, in surprise.

"Yes," said Joshua. "Nichols got tired waiting for you, so I told him I'd stay till you got back."

"I had some distance to go, and that detained me. Did you have any customers?"

"Yes, I just sold a spool of cotton to a little girl."

"I met her a little way up the road, holding the spool in her hand."

"Well," said Joshua, "I guess I'll go, now you've got back."

He went across the street to his father's house, and, going up into his own room, locked the door, not wishing to be interrupted. Then, opening his desk, he took out a sheet of paper, and wrote a note to the address given in his lottery circular, requesting the parties to send him by return of mail a lottery ticket. He added, shrewdly as he thought, "If this ticket draws a prize, I will keep on buying; but if it don't I shall get discouraged and stop."

"I guess that'll fetch 'em," thought Joshua. He folded up the paper, and, inclosing the bill, directed it.

The next thing to do was to mail it.

Now this seemed a very simple thing, but it really occasioned considerable trouble. The postmaster in a small village can generally identify many of the correspondents who send letters through his office by their handwriting. He knew Joshua's, and such a letter as this would attract his attention and set him to gossiping. Considering the circumstances under which he obtained the money, this was hardly desirable, and Joshua therefore decided, though unwillingly, on account of the trouble, to walk to the next post-office, a distance of three miles, and post his letter there.

He came downstairs with his letter in his pocket. "Where are you going, Joshua?" asked his mother.

"Going out to walk," said Joshua, shortly.

"I wanted to send a little bundle to Mr. Faulkner's, but that is too far off."

"I'll carry it," said Joshua.

Mrs. Drummond was astonished at this unusual spirit of accommodation, for Joshua was, in general, far from obliging. The truth was, however, that, though Mr. Faulkner lived over a mile and a quarter distant, it was on his way to the post-office.

"Thank you, Joshua," said Mrs. Drummond. "I was afraid you wouldn't be willing to go so far."

"I feel just like taking a long walk to-day, mother."

"Here is the bundle. I will bake a little pie for you while you are gone."

So things seemed to be working very smoothly for Joshua, and he set out on his three-mile walk in very good spirits. His walk he knew would make him hungry, and the pie which his mother promised him would be very acceptable on his return.

Arrived in front of Mr. Faulkner's, he saw Frank Faulkner, a boy of twelve, playing outside.

"Frank," called out Joshua, "here's a bundle I want you to carry into the house. Tell your folks my mother sent it."

"All right," said Frank, and he carried it in.

Joshua proceeded on his way, and finally reached the post-office.

"Give me a three-cent postage-stamp," he said to the postmaster.

This was speedily affixed to the letter, and, after resting a short time, he set out on his walk homeward.

Reaching the house of Mr. Faulkner, he was hailed by Frank, who was still playing outside.

"Where have you been, Joshua?"

Joshua was not desirous of having it known where he had been, and he answered, in the surly manner characteristic of him, "What business is that of yours?"

"Where did you learn manners?" asked Frank, who was a sturdy scion of Young America, and quite disposed to stand up for his rights.

"If you're impudent, I'll give you a licking," growled Joshua.

"Next time you come along this way, you may take in your own bundles," retorted Frank.

"If I had a stick, I'd give you something you wouldn't like."

"You'd have to catch me first," said Frank.

Joshua's temper, which was none of the sweetest, was by this time roused, and he started in pursuit of Frank, but the younger boy dodged so adroitly as to baffle his pursuit. In attempting to catch him, indeed, Joshua stubbed his toe violently against a projecting root, and measured his length by the roadside.

"Who's down, I wonder?" asked Frank, scrambling over the fence, where he felt safe.

"I'll wring your neck some time, you young imp!" exclaimed Joshua, gathering himself up slowly and painfully, and shaking his fist vindictively at Frank.

"I'll wait till you're ready," returned Frank. "I'm in no hurry."

At length Joshua reached home, feeling tired and provoked, but congratulating himself that he had taken the first step towards the grand prize which loomed in dazzling prospect before his eyes.

CHAPTER XVII. JOSHUA'S DISAPPOINTMENT.

In due time, to Joshua's great delight, the lottery ticket reached him. It was several days in coming, and he had almost given it up, but the sight of it raised his spirits to the highest pitch. It seemed to him the first step to a fortune. He began at once to indulge in dazzling visions of what he would do when the prize came to hand; how the "old man" would be astonished and treat him with increased respect; how he would go to the city and have a good time seeing the lions, and from henceforth throw off the galling yoke of dependence which his father's parsimony had made it so hard to bear.

Whenever he was by himself, he used to pull out the ticket and gaze at it with the greatest satisfaction, as the key that was to unlock the portals of Fortune, Independence, and Happiness.

He had been afraid that his appropriation of five dollars would be detected, and every time his father entered the house he looked into his face with some apprehension; but days rolled by, and nothing was heard. He congratulated himself that he had been able to sell the shawl for precisely the sum he needed, otherwise the money might have been missed that very night. As it was, neither the shawl nor the bill had been missed.

About this time he received a letter from Sam Crawford, describing the gayeties of the city. It closed thus:—

"By the way, Josh, when are you coming up to the city, to take a look at the lions? It's a shame that a young man of your age should be cooped up in an insignificant little village like Stapleton. I wouldn't exchange the knowledge of the world I have obtained here for five hundred dollars! What a green rustic I was when I first came here! But it didn't take me long to find the way round, and now I know the ropes as well as the next man. I generally play billiards in the evening, and, if I do say it myself, I am rather hard to beat. When you come up, I'll give you a few lessons. I can't help pitying you for leading such a slow, humdrum life in the country. I should be moped to death if I were in your place. Can't you induce the old man to fork over the stamps, and come up here, if only for a week?"

This letter had the effect of making Joshua very much disgusted with Stapleton. Brilliant visions of city life and city enjoyments flitted before his eyes, and he felt that nothing was needed to make a man of him except the knowledge of life which a city residence would be sure to give.

"It's all true what Sam says," he soliloquized. "A man can't learn anything of life here. No wonder he looks upon me as a green rustic. How can I be anything else in this miserable little village? But as for the old man's paying my expenses on a visit, he's too mean for that. But then there is the lottery ticket. Just as soon as I get hold of my prize, I'll go on my own hook."

I append a passage from Joshua's reply to Sam's letter:—

"There isn't any chance of the old man's forking over stamps enough to pay for my visit to New York. He's too thundering mean for that. All he cares for is to make money. *But I'm coming, for all that.* I've bought a lottery ticket, as you advised, and just as soon as I get hold of the prize, I shall come and make you a visit. I should like very much to learn billiards. I wish there was a billiard table in Stapleton, though it wouldn't do me much good if there were, the old man keeps me so close. I shall be glad when I am twenty-one. I don't see why he can't let me have a few thousand dollars then, and set me up in business in the city. Perhaps we could go in together as partners. However, there is no use in talking about him, for he won't do it. *But I may get hold of the money some other way.* Would five thousand dollars be enough to set a fellow up in business in New York?

"You will hear from me again soon. I hope I shall be able to write you that I am coming to see you.

"Your friend,
"Joshua Drummond."

It will be seen that Joshua was willing to go into business for himself, though he did not care to take a situation. He had the idea, which I think is entertained by a large number of boys and young men, that an employer has nothing to do but to sit at his desk, count over his money, and order his clerks around. For such an employment as this Joshua felt that he was well adapted, and would very much have enjoyed the sense of importance it would give him. But Joshua made a great mistake. Many employers look back upon the years which they passed as clerks as years of comparative leisure and ease, certainly of freedom from anxiety. They find that they have a heavy price to pay for the privilege of being their own masters, and the masters of others. But Joshua was thoroughly lazy, and it was this feeling that dictated the wish which he expressed in his letter to Sam Crawford.

The days passed very slowly, it must be acknowledged. Joshua was in a restless and excited state. Though he expected to draw a prize, he knew that there was a remote chance of failing to draw anything, and he wanted the matter decided.

But at length the long-expected letter arrived. Joshua did not like to open it in the post-office, lest it should attract the attention of the postmaster. He therefore withdrew to a place where he was not likely to be disturbed, and with trembling fingers opened the letter.

Something dropped out.

"I wonder if it is a check?" thought Joshua, stooping over and picking it up.

But no, it was an announcement of the drawing.

Joshua's numbers,—for each lottery ticket contains three numbers,—were 9, 15, 50. But of the thirteen lucky numbers drawn out of sixty-five, neither of them was one.

Slowly it dawned upon Joshua that he had drawn nothing, that his five dollars had been absolutely thrown away. But there was a letter. Perhaps this would explain it.

Joshua read as follows:—

"Dear Sir:—We regret to say that we are unable to send you a prize this time. We hope, however, you will not be discouraged. Some of our patrons who have been most fortunate have commenced by being unlucky. Indeed, singularly enough, this is a general rule. Let us cite an instance. Mr. B——, of your State, bought his first ticket of us last spring. It turned out a blank. We wrote him not to be discouraged, but we did not hear from him for some weeks. Finally he sent us a remittance for a ticket, adding that he sent it with a very faint hope of success. He was convinced that he was born to ill-luck. But what was the result? In less than a fortnight we had the pleasure and gratification of sending him five thousand dollars, minus our usual commission. Suppose he had been discouraged by a first failure, you can see how much he would have lost.

"Hoping to hear from you again, and to send you in return better news, we subscribe ourselves,

"Very respectfully,

"Grabb & Co."

The effect of Joshua's ill success was to make him very despondent.

"It's all very well to say 'Try again,'" he said to himself, "but where can I get the money? That five dollars is thrown away, and I've got nothing to show for it."

He thought of all he had intended to do, and now his castles had crumbled, and all in consequence of this letter. He had been so sanguine of success. Now he must write to Sam that his visit to New York was indefinitely postponed, that is, unless he could induce his father to provide him with money enough to go. The prospect was not very encouraging, but he felt desperate, and he determined to make the attempt.

Accordingly, just after supper, he detained his father, just as he was returning to the store, and said:—

"Father, I wish you'd let me go to New York on a visit."

"What for?" asked Mr. Drummond, elevating his brows.

"Because I'm eighteen years old, and I've never been there yet."

"Then, if you've gone eighteen years without seeing the city, I think you can go a while longer," said his father, under the impression that he had made a witty remark. But Joshua did not appreciate the humor of it.

"I've lived in Stapleton ever since I was born," grumbled Joshua, "and have got tired of it. I want to see something of life."

"Do you? Well, I'm sure I've no objection."

"May I go then?"

"Yes."

"When?" asked Joshua, joyfully.

"To-morrow, if you like; but of course you will pay your own expenses."

"How can I?" exclaimed Joshua, in angry disappointment. "I have no money."

"Then you can save up your allowance till you have enough."

"Save up on twenty-five cents a week! I couldn't go till I was an old man!"

"I know of no other way," said Mr. Drummond, with provoking indifference, "unless you earn the money in some way."

"You treat me like a little boy!" said Joshua, angrily.

"You are better off than I am. I have to work for all I get. You get your board, clothes, and pocket-money for nothing."

"Other boys go to New York when they are much younger."

"I have told you you can go when you like, but you mustn't expect me to supply the money."

Mr. Drummond put on his hat and crossed the street to the store, leaving Joshua in a very unfilial frame of mind.

CHAPTER XVIII. WALTER FINDS HIMSELF IN HOT WATER.

Two days later two women entered Mr. Drummond's store. One was Joshua's customer, and she wore the same shawl which she had purchased of him.

It happened that Walter was out, but Mr. Drummond and Nichols were both behind the counter.

"Have you got any more shawls like this?" asked the first lady, whom we will call Mrs. Blake. "Mrs. Spicer, who is a neighbor of mine, liked it so well that she wants to get another just like it."

This was addressed to Mr. Drummond, who happened to be nearest the door.

"Did you buy this shawl of us?" asked Mr. Drummond.

"Yes, sir. I bought it about a fortnight ago, and paid five dollars for it."

"Five dollars! There must be some mistake. We never sell such a shawl as that for less than ten dollars."

"I can't help it," said Mrs. Blake, positively. "I bought it here, and paid five dollars for it."

"Why, those shawls cost me seven dollars and a half at wholesale. It is not likely I would sell them for five."

"I didn't buy it of you."

"Mr. Nichols," said Mr. Drummond, "did you sell this lady the shawl she is wearing, for five dollars?"

"No, sir; have not sold a shawl like that for two months. I know the price well enough, and I wouldn't sell it for less than ten dollars."

"I didn't buy it of him, I bought it of a boy," said Mrs. Blake.

"It must have been that stupid Conrad," exclaimed Mr. Drummond, angrily. "Wait till he comes in, and I'll haul him over the coals."

"Then you won't let my friend have another like it for

five dollars?"

"No," said Mr. Drummond, provoked. "I don't do business that way. I've lost nearly three dollars by that shawl of yours. You ought to make up the wholesale price to me."

"I shan't do it," said Mrs. Blake. "If you've made a mistake, it's your lookout. I wasn't willing to pay more than five dollars."

The two ladies were about to leave the store when Mr. Drummond said, "The boy will be back directly. I wish you would wait a few minutes, so that if he denies it you can prove it upon him."

"I've got a call to make," said Mrs. Blake, "but I'll come in again in about an hour."

They left the store, and Mr. Drummond began to berate the absent Walter. He was provoked to find that he had lost two dollars and a half, and, if Walter had been in receipt of any wages, would have stopped the amount out of his salary. But, unfortunately for this plan of reprisal, our hero received his board only, and that could not very well be levied upon. However, he might have some money in his possession, and Mr. Drummond decided to require him to make up the loss.

"When did she say she bought the shawl, Mr. Nichols?" asked his employer.

"About a fortnight ago."

"Will you look on the books, and see if you find the sale recorded? I am surprised that it escaped my attention."

Nichols looked over the book of sales, and announced that no such entry could be found.

Mr. Drummond was surprised. Though not inclined to judge others any too charitably, he had never suspected Walter of dishonesty.

"Are you sure you looked back far enough?" he asked.

"Yes," said Nichols; "to make sure, I looked back four

weeks. The woman said only a fortnight, you know."

"I know. Then it seems Conrad has concealed the sale and kept the money."

"Perhaps," suggested Nichols, who rather liked Walter, "he forgot to put it down."

"If he did, he forgot to put the money in the drawer, for the cash and the sales have always balanced. He's an ungrateful young rascal," continued Mr. Drummond, harshly. "After I took him into my house and treated him as a son (this was not saying much, if Joshua may be believed), he has robbed me in the most cold-blooded manner."

Why there should be anything cold-blooded in appropriating the price of the shawl, even had the charge been true, I cannot say, nor could Mr. Drummond probably, but he thought that the use of this term would make the offence seem more aggravated.

Even Nichols was a little staggered by the evidence against our hero. He did not like to think him guilty, but it certainly seemed as if he must be.

"What are you going to do about it, Mr. Drummond?" he asked.

"I suppose I ought to have him arrested. He deserves it."

"I hope you won't do that. He may be able to explain it."

"If I do not proceed to extremities, it will be on account of his relationship, which I blush to acknowledge."

The time had been, and that not long since, when Mr. Drummond felt proud of his relationship to the rich Squire Conrad of Willoughby; but that was before his loss of property. Circumstances alter cases.

Quite unconscious of the storm that was gathering, Walter at this moment entered the store.

"So you've got back!" said Mr. Drummond, harshly.

"Yes, sir."

"You haven't been in any particular hurry. However, that was not what I wished to speak to you about. We have made a discovery since you went out."

"Have you, sir?" asked Walter, rather surprised by the peculiar tone which Mr. Drummond saw fit to adopt.

"Yes, and not a very agreeable one."

"I am sorry for that," said Walter, not knowing what else was expected of him.

"No doubt you are sorry," sneered Mr. Drummond. "I should think he would be, eh, Mr. Nichols?"

"I am sorry also," said Nichols, who, though rather weak-minded, was a good-hearted young man.

"So am I sorry," said Mr. Drummond. "It strikes me I have most reason to be sorry, considering that the loss has fallen on me."

All this was an enigma to Walter, and he had not the faintest idea of what his employer meant. He inferred, however, that some blame was about to be laid upon him.

"If you have no objection, Mr. Drummond," he said quietly, "perhaps you will tell me what has happened."

"I have found out your ingratitude, Conrad," said Mr. Drummond, preparing for a lecture, which he rather liked to indulge in, as his wife could have testified. "I have discovered how like a viper you have repaid me for my kindness. You didn't think I would find out, but your iniquity has providentially come to light. While I was loading you with benefits, you prepared to sting the hand of your benefactor."

"I don't know what you are talking about, Mr. Drummond," said Walter, impatiently. "I wish you would stop talking in riddles, and let me know in what way I resemble a viper."

"Did you ever witness such brazen effrontery, Mr. Nichols?" demanded Mr. Drummond, turning to his head salesman; "even when he is found out, he brazens it out."

"Wouldn't it be as well to tell him what is the matter, Mr. Drummond?" asked Nichols, who was in hopes our hero would be able to prove his innocence.

"Won't you tell me, Mr. Nichols?" asked Walter.

"No," said Mr. Drummond, waving his hand; "it is my duty to tell him myself. I will do so briefly. Walter Conrad, when I admitted you into my house I little dreamed that I was harboring a thief."

"A thief!" exclaimed Walter, his eyes flashing with anger, and elevating his fist involuntarily. "Who dares to call me a thief?"

"No violence, Conrad," said Mr. Drummond. "Such a theatrical display of indignation and surprise won't help you any. We are not to be imposed upon by your artful demonstrations."

"Mr. Drummond," burst forth Walter, fairly aroused, "you are insulting me by every word you speak. I am no more a thief than you are."

"Do you call me a thief?" exclaimed Mr. Drummond, turning white about the lips.

"No, I don't; but I have as much right to call you one as you have to charge such a thing upon me."

"I can prove what I say," said his employer. "I have got you in a net."

"It won't take me long to get out of any net you may set for me. I insist upon your telling me at once what you mean."

"This language is rather extraordinary for a boy convicted of dishonesty to use towards his employer."

"I am not convicted of dishonesty. Mr. Nichols, I appeal to you to tell me, what Mr. Drummond does not seem disposed to do, what is the meaning of this false charge which he has trumped up against me."

"I am sure you can prove your innocence, Conrad," said Nichols, soothingly.

"Mr. Nichols, will you do me the favor to be silent?" said his employer, sharply. "The matter concerns Conrad and myself, and I don't choose that any one should communicate with him except myself. To come to the point, did you, or did you not, a fortnight since, sell one of those shawls, such as you see on the counter, for five dollars?"

"I did not," said Walter, promptly.

"It might not have been exactly a fortnight. Have you sold such a shawl within four weeks?"

"I have not sold such a shawl since I have been in your employ, Mr. Drummond."

"You hear what he says, Mr. Nichols," said Mr. Drummond. "You see how he adds falsehood to dishonesty. But that is not uncommon. It is only what I expected. Do you mean to say, Walter Conrad, that you didn't sell such a shawl for five dollars (only half price), and, instead of entering the sale, put the money into your own pocket?"

"I do deny it most emphatically, Mr. Drummond," said Walter, impetuously, "and I challenge you to prove it."

CHAPTER XIX. THE TABLES ARE TURNED.

"I shall soon be able to prove it," said Mr. Drummond. "The lady who bought the shawl came into the store half an hour since, and asked for another. When I told her that it would cost ten dollars, she said she only paid five for the one she had on. She then told us that she bought it of you a fortnight since."

"How did she know my name?"

"She did not mention your name. She said that it was a boy she bought it of, and of course that can only be you."

"There is some mistake about this, Mr. Drummond. She has made a mistake. She must have bought it somewhere else."

"She would not be likely to make such a mistake as this. Besides, the shawl is like others I have. How do you account for that?" queried Mr. Drummond, triumphantly.

"I don't pretend to account for it, and don't feel called upon to do so. All I have got to say is, that I did not sell the shawl, nor pocket the money."

"I shouldn't be surprised if you had the money about you at this very moment."

"You are mistaken," said Walter, firmly.

"Show me your pocket-book."

"My pocket-book is my own property."

"You are afraid to show it. Observe that, Mr. Nichols. Does not that look like guilt?"

"I am willing to show it to Mr. Nichols," said Walter.

He took it from his pocket, and handed it to Nichols, who took it rather unwillingly.

"Open that pocket-book, Mr. Nichols, and show me what is in it."

"Shall I do so, Walter?" asked Nichols.

"Yes, Mr. Nichols. There is nothing in it that I am ashamed of."

Nichols opened the pocket-book and took out three bills.

"What are those bills, Mr. Nichols?" asked his employer.

"There is a one, here is a two, and here is—" Nichols hesitated and looked disturbed—"here is a five."

Mr. Drummond's mean face was radiant with exultation.

"I told you so. I think we need no further proof. The stolen money has been found in Conrad's possession, and his falsehood and dishonesty are clearly proved. Hand me that five."

"Stop a minute, Mr. Drummond," said Walter, coolly. "You are altogether too much in a hurry. You have proved nothing whatever. That five-dollar bill I brought from home with me, and I have kept it ever since, having no occasion to spend it."

"Do you think I will believe any such story?" asked his employer, with a sneer. "That is very plausible, Conrad, but very improbable. I have no doubt whatever that the bill is the same one which was paid you for the shawl."

"Then you are entirely mistaken."

"That remains to be seen. Mr. Nichols, I will relieve you of that pocket-book. As the shawl should have been sold for ten dollars, the entire contents will not be sufficient to pay for the loss I have sustained."

"Mr. Nichols," said Walter, "I forbid your giving that pocket-book to Mr. Drummond. He has no claim to it whatever. You may give it to me."

"I forbid you giving it to Conrad," broke in his employer.

"I don't know what to do," said Nichols, perplexed, looking from one to the other.

"You know that it belongs to me, Mr. Nichols," said Walter.

"I—I think I had better lay it down on the counter," said Nichols, by the way of compromise.

Walter, who was on the outside, sprang to the counter, and seized it just in time to prevent Mr. Drummond's obtaining it. The latter was very angry at his want of success, and exclaimed violently, "Walter Conrad, give me that pocket-book instantly."

Walter, who had put it in an inside pocket of his coat, coolly buttoned the coat and answered, "If you had any claim to it, Mr. Drummond, you would not have to speak twice; but as it is mine, I prefer to keep it."

Mr. Drummond, though he had an irritable, aggravating temper, was not one to proceed to violence on ordinary occasions. But just now he was thoroughly provoked, and showed it. He sprang over the counter with an agility worthy of his youth, and advanced threateningly upon Walter.

"Walter Conrad," he exclaimed furiously, "how dare you defy me in this outrageous manner? Do you know that I can have you arrested; but in consideration of your being a relation, I may be induced to spare you the penalty of the law if you will give me what money you have towards making up my loss."

"So I would, if the loss had come through me. But I have already told you that this is not the case. I know nothing whatever about the shawl."

"And this," said Mr. Drummond, folding his arms, "this is the viper that I have warmed in my bosom. This is the friendless orphan that I admitted beneath my roof, and made a companion of my son. This is the ungrateful serpent who has crept into my confidence, and abused it!"

Mr. Drummond was an orator on a small scale, and the pleasure of giving utterance to this scathing denunciation caused him to delay his intention to obtain possession of the pocket-book by violence.

Walter ought to have been withered by this outburst of righteous anger, but he wasn't. He stood it very well, and did not seem in the least affected.

"Behold his hardened effrontery, Mr. Nichols," pursued Mr. Drummond, unfolding his arms, and pointing at our hero with quivering fore-finger. "I could not have believed that a boy of his years could be so brazen."

"Mr. Drummond," said Walter, "I am sustained by a

consciousness of my innocence, and therefore what you say has no effect upon me. It doesn't seem to be very just to convict me without evidence, and sentence me without trial."

"Will you give up that pocket-book?" demanded Mr. Drummond, furiously, having indulged in his little flight of oratory, and being now ready to proceed to business.

"No, sir, I will not," returned Walter, looking him firmly in the face.

Mr. Drummond made a dash for him, but Walter was used to dodging, and, eluding his grasp, ran behind the counter.

"Mr. Nichols, help me to catch him," said Mr. Drummond, quite red in the face.

But Nichols did not show any great readiness to obey. He let Walter pass him, and did not make the least effort to retain him.

Mr. Drummond was making ready to jump over the counter, when Nichols, to his great relief, observed the ladies, already referred to, coming up the steps from the street.

"Mr. Drummond, the ladies have returned," he said hastily.

"Aha!" said his employer, with exultation. "Now we will be able to prove your guilt, you young rascal! Here is the lady who bought the shawl of you."

Mrs. Blake and her friend, Mrs. Spicer, here entered the store.

Mr. Drummond went forward to meet them. His face was flushed, but he tried to look composed.

"I am glad to see you back, ladies," he said. "You told me that you bought your shawl of a boy?" turning to Mrs. Blake.

"Yes, sir."

"Come forward, Conrad," said Mr. Drummond, a malignant smile overspreading his face. "Perhaps you will deny now, to this lady's face, that you sold her the shawl she has on."

"I certainly do," said Walter. "I never, to my knowledge, saw the lady before, and I know that I did not sell her the shawl."

"What do you think of that, Mr. Nichols?" said Mr. Drummond. "Did you ever witness such unblushing falsehood?"

But here a shell was thrown into Mr. Drummond's camp, and by Mrs. Blake herself.

"The boy is perfectly right," she said. "I did not buy the shawl of him."

"What!" stammered Mr. Drummond.

Mrs. Blake repeated her statement.

"Didn't you say you bought the shawl of the boy?" asked Mr. Drummond, with a sickly hue of disappointment overspreading his face.

"Yes, but it was not that boy."

"That is the only boy I have in my employment."

"Come to think of it, I believe it was your son," said Mrs. Blake. "Isn't he a little older than this boy?"

"My son,—Joshua!" exclaimed Mr. Drummond.

"Yes, I think it must be he. He's got rather an old-looking face, with freckles and reddish hair; isn't so good-looking as this boy."

"Joshua!" repeated Mr. Drummond, bewildered. "He doesn't tend in the store."

"It was about dinner-time," said Mrs. Blake. "He was the only one here."

"Do you know anything about this, Mr. Nichols?" asked Mr. Drummond, turning to his head clerk.

Light had dawned upon Nichols. He remembered now Joshua's offer to take his place, and he felt sure in his own mind who was the guilty party.

"Yes, Mr. Drummond," he answered; "about a fortnight ago, as Walter was rather late in getting back, Joshua offered to stay in the store for a while. He must have sold the shawl, but he must have guessed at the price."

"A mistake has been made," said Mr. Drummond, hurriedly, to the ladies,—"a mistake that you have profited by. I shall not be able to sell you another shawl for less than ten dollars."

The ladies went out, and Mr. Drummond and his two clerks were left alone.

"Mr. Drummond," said Walter, quietly, "after what has happened, you will not be surprised if I decline to remain in your employ. I shall take the afternoon train to Willoughby."

He walked out of the store, and crossed the street to Mr. Drummond's house.

CHAPTER XX. IN WHICH JOSHUA COMES TO GRIEF.

Walter went up to his room, and hastily packed his trunk. He felt wronged and outraged by the unfounded charge that had been made against him. Why, he argued, should Mr. Drummond so readily decide that he had cheated him out of five dollars? He felt that he could not, with any self-respect, remain any longer under the same roof with a man who had such a poor opinion of him.

He was not sorry that his engagement was at an end. He had obtained some knowledge of the dry-goods business, and he knew that his services were worth more than his board. Then again, though he was not particular about living luxuriously, the fare at Mr. Drummond's was so uncommonly poor that he did sometimes long for one of the abundant and well-cooked meals which he used to have spread before him at home, or even at his boarding-house while a pupil of the Essex Classical Institute.

He was packing his trunk when a step was heard on the stairs, and his door was opened by Mr. Drummond, considerably to Walter's surprise.

The fact is, that Mr. Drummond, on realizing what a mistake he had made, and that Joshua was the real culprit, felt that he had gone altogether too far, and he realized that he would be severely censured by Walter's friends in Willoughby. Besides, it was just possible that Walter might, after all, recover a few thousand dollars from his father's estate, and therefore it was better to be on good terms with him. Mr. Drummond determined, therefore, to conciliate Walter, and induce him, if possible, to remain in his house and employ.

"What are you doing, Conrad?" he asked, on entering Walter's chamber.

"Packing my trunk, sir," said Walter.

"Surely you are not going to leave us."

"I think it best," said Walter, quietly.

"You won't—ahem!—bear malice on account of the little

mistake I made. We are all liable to mistakes."

"It was something more than a mistake, Mr. Drummond. What had you seen in me to justify you in such a sudden charge of dishonesty?"

"Almost anybody would have been deceived under the circumstances," said Mr. Drummond, awkwardly.

"You did not give me an opportunity to defend myself, or rather you disbelieved all I said."

"Well, Conrad, I was mistaken. I shall be glad to have you come back to the store as before."

"Thank you, Mr. Drummond, but I have decided to go back to Willoughby for a short time. I want to consult Mr. Shaw about the future. It is time I formed some plans, as I shall probably have to earn my living."

"Don't you think you had better wait a few months?"

"No, sir, I think not."

"If you have made up your mind, all I have to say is that my humble dwelling will be ever open to receive you in the future. Perhaps, after a short visit at your old home, you may feel inclined to return to my employment. I will give you a dollar a week besides board."

Mr. Drummond looked as if he felt that this was a magnificent offer, for which Walter ought to feel grateful. But our hero knew very well that he could command better pay elsewhere, and was not particularly impressed. Still he wished to be polite.

"Thank you for your offer, Mr. Drummond," he said; "but I am not prepared to say, as yet, what I will do."

"I hope," said Mr. Drummond, rather embarrassed, "you won't speak of our little difference to your friends at Willoughby."

"No, sir, not if you wish me not to do so."

By this time the trunk was packed, and Walter, locking it, rose from his knees.

"If it won't be too much trouble, Mr. Drummond," he said, "I will send for my trunk to-morrow."

"Certainly. Why won't you wait till to-morrow yourself?"

"As I am ready, I may as well take the afternoon train."

"Very well; just as you think best."

"I will go down and bid good-by to Mrs. Drummond."

Mrs. Drummond had just come from the kitchen. She looked with surprise at Walter and her husband, whose presence in the house at that hour was unusual.

"What is the matter?" she asked.

"Conrad is going home a short time on business," explained Mr. Drummond.

"When shall we see you back again, Walter?" asked Mrs. Drummond.

"That is uncertain," said Walter. "It depends upon my plans for the future."

"I have offered him increased pay," said Mr. Drummond, "if he will return to the store. I hope he may decide to do so. Our humble roof will ever be ready to shelter him."

Considering that Mr. Drummond had not lately made any such hospitable references to the humble roof, his wife looked somewhat puzzled.

Just at that moment Joshua, unconscious of the damaging discovery that had been made relative to himself, entered the room.

"Hallo! what's up?" he asked.

It was the first time his father had seen him since the discovery of his dishonesty, and his anger was kindled.

"You ought to be ashamed to show your face here, you young reprobate!" he exclaimed.

Joshua stared in amazement, and Mrs. Drummond

exclaimed, "What makes you talk so, Mr. Drummond? What has he done?"

"What has he done?" ejaculated Mr. Drummond, adding, rather ungrammatically, "He's a thief, that's what he's done."

"How can you say such things of your own son?"

"Shut up, Mrs. Drummond; you don't know what you're talking about, or you wouldn't defend him. It would serve him right if I should flog him within an inch of his life."

"If you try it," said Joshua, sullenly, "I'll have you arrested for assault and battery."

"Take care, boy! or you may find yourself in custody for theft."

"What do all these dreadful words mean?" asked Mrs. Drummond, distressed. "Tell me, Walter, if you know."

"I would rather Mr. Drummond informed you," said Walter.

"I'll tell you, Mrs. Drummond," said her husband. "That boy sold a shawl a fortnight ago, when alone in the store, and pocketed the money."

"Who said I did?" asked Joshua, boldly, though he looked a little pale.

"The woman who bought it of you was in the store to-day."

"Did she say I sold it to her?"

"Yes."

"Did she know my name?"

"No, but she described you."

"So I did," said Joshua, finding it advisable to remember. "I remember now I sold it for five dollars."

"What made you keep the money?"

"I didn't. I waited till Conrad came into the store, and gave the money to him. What he did with it, I don't know. Perhaps he forgot to put it in the drawer," he added, with a spiteful look at Walter.

"That's a lie, Joshua Drummond!" said Walter, quietly, "and you know it is. I think your father knows it is also."

"Do you mean to say I lie?" blustered Joshua.

"I wouldn't if I wasn't obliged to; but in my own defence I am compelled to do so."

"What could I want of the money?" demanded Joshua, with a look of virtuous indignation.

"I might as well ask the same question of myself; but that would be a poor defence. If you really want me to answer that question, I will do it."

"Go ahead, then," said Joshua. "I hope my word is better than that of a beggar living on charity."

"Joshua!" said his mother, in a tone of remonstrance.

"I think you wanted the money to buy lottery tickets with," said Walter, calmly.

Joshua turned pale, and looked thunderstruck.

"To buy lottery tickets with!" he gasped, staring at Walter in dismay.

"What's that?" asked Mr. Drummond, pricking up his ears.

"Your son can tell you," said Walter.

"What does this mean, Joshua?" demanded his father, sternly.

"It's a lie," said Joshua, unblushingly.

"Have you bought no lottery tickets?"

"No."

"Can you prove this charge which you have made against my son?" asked Mr. Drummond, turning to Walter.

"I can, but I am sorry to do so. I picked up this letter a day or two since, and intended to give it back to Joshua, but it escaped my mind. I would not have exposed him if he had not tried to charge me with theft."

He placed in Mr. Drummond's hands the letter already given, announcing to Joshua that he had drawn a blank.

Mr. Drummond read it with no little anger, for he detested lotteries.

"Unhappy boy!" he said, addressing Joshua. "I understand now what became of the five dollars. This decides me to do what I had intended to do sooner. I have supported you in laziness long enough. It is time you went to work. Next week you must go to work. I will take you into my store; but as I am not sure of your honesty, if I find you appropriating money to your own use, I will put you into a shoe-shop and make a shoemaker of you."

This was an alarming threat to Joshua, who had a foolish pride, which led him to look upon a trade as less respectable than the mercantile profession. He slunk out of the house, and Mr. Drummond went back to the store, while Walter set out on foot for the railway station, three-quarters of a mile distant.

CHAPTER XXI. A NEW ACQUAINTANCE.

"Give me a ticket to Willoughby," said Walter, offering the five-dollar bill which he had come so near losing.

The ticket was handed him, and three dollars and seventy-five cents were returned to him.

"How long are you going to stay away?" asked the station-master, with whom Walter had some acquaintance.

"I may not come back at all."

"Have you left Drummond's store?"

"Yes."

"Isn't that rather sudden?"

"A little so; but I didn't mean to stay long."

The shriek of the locomotive now became audible, and Walter went out on the platform. Five minutes later found him occupying a seat, or rather half a seat, for there sat next to him a brisk, energetic-looking man, of about thirty years of age.

He had been reading the morning paper, but apparently he had got through with it, for he folded it up, and put it in his pocket.

"Fine day," he said, briskly.

"Yes, sir, very fine," answered Walter.

"Some people are affected by the weather; I am not," pursued his fellow-traveller. "I feel as smart one day as another."

"It isn't quite so cheerful when it rains," observed Walter.

"I'm always cheerful. I've got too much business to do to mope. When a man's got enough to busy himself about, he hasn't time to be in the dumps."

"There's a good deal in that," said Walter.

"Of course there is. Push along, keep moving, that's my motto. Are you in business?"

"No, sir, not at present."

"I'm in the subscription-book business,—got an office in New York. We send out agents everywhere to canvass for our publication. Lots of money in it."

"Is there?"

"Yes. I used to be an agent myself, and, though I say it, I don't think there are many agents that can get ahead of me. Sometimes I used to make twenty dollars a day. At last I thought I'd like to settle down, so I bought a partnership, and now, instead of being an agent, I send out agents."

"Isn't twenty dollars a day pretty large for an agent to make?" asked Walter.

"Yes, there are not many do it, but plenty make from five to ten right along. You look as if you would make a good agent."

"What makes you think so?" asked Walter.

"You look smart."

"Thank you," said Walter, laughing. "I am afraid you won't think so much of my ability when I tell you I have been working for the last three months for my board."

"It's a shame. You'd better come with us. We'll do much better by you than that."

"I am going to consult some friends about my future plans. If you are willing to tell me a little of your business, I will think of what you propose."

"I have with me our latest publication. It's going like wildfire. Just the thing to please the people. I'll show it to you."

Walter looked with interest while his new acquaintance drew out from a carpet-bag, which he had beneath the seat, a good-sized parcel wrapped in brown paper. Untying it, he produced a bulky octavo, in flashy binding, and abounding in illustrations. He opened the book and turned over the leaves rapidly.

"It's stuffed full of illustrations, you see," said he. "The expense of the pictures alone was absolutely e-nor-mous!" he added, dwelling upon the last word by way of emphasis. "But we're going to make it pay. The sale will be immense. Our agents already in the field report remarkable sales."

"What's the title of the book?" asked Walter, who had yet

been unable to determine this point, by reason of the rapid turning of the pages.

"'Scenes in Bible Lands.' We include other countries besides Palestine, and we've made a book that'll sell. Most every family will want one."

"What terms do you offer to agents?"

"Why, the book sells at retail at three dollars and fifty cents. Of this the agent keeps one dollar and twenty-five cents. Pretty good, isn't it?"

"Yes, I should think it was."

"You see you have only to sell four copies a day to make five dollars. If you're smart, you can do better than that."

It really did seem very good to Walter, who couldn't help comparing it with the miserable wages he had received from Mr. Drummond.

"I think that would pay very well," he said.

"Most paying business out," said the other. "Say the word, and I'll engage you on the spot."

"Where would you want me to sell?"

"I should like to have you go West. This way districts are mostly taken up. It would give you a good chance to travel and see the world."

Now Walter was, like most young people, fond of new scenes, and this consideration was a weighty one. It would enable him to travel, and pay his expenses while doing so.

"Better say the word."

"I can't now. I must see my friends first."

"Where are you going?"

"To Willoughby."

"How long are you going to stay?"

"I can't tell. A few days probably."

"Well, I'll give you the number of our office in New York. When you get ready, report to us there, and we'll put you in the field."

To this Walter assented, and asked several questions further, to which he received encouraging answers. The stranger gave him his card, from which our hero learned that he had made the acquaintance of Mr. James Pusher, of the firm of Flint & Pusher, subscription publishers, No. — Nassau St., New York.

"Good-by," said Mr. Pusher, cordially, when Walter left the train for the Willoughby station; "hope to see you again."

"Thank you," said Walter; "very likely you will."

Taking his carpet-bag in his hand, for he had arranged to have his trunk come the next day, he walked over to the house of Mr. Shaw, his father's executor.

Mr. Shaw was in his office, a little one-story building standing by itself a little to the left of his house. He was busily writing, and did not at once look up. When he saw who it was, he rose up and welcomed Walter with a smile.

"I'm very glad to see you, Walter," he said. "I was just wishing you were here. When did you leave Stapleton?"

"This afternoon, Mr. Shaw. I have just reached Willoughby."

"And how did you like Stapleton?"

"Tolerably well."

"And Mr. Drummond,—how were you pleased with him?"

"As to that," said Walter, smiling, "I can't say that I liked him as well as I might."

"I judged that from what I have heard of his character. He has the reputation of being very mean. A cent in his eyes is as large as a dollar appears to some men. How did he pay you for your services?"

"I worked for board wages."

"And pretty poor board at that, I imagine."

"I had no fear of the gout," said Walter. "The living isn't luxurious."

"Well, I'm glad you are back again. For the present I shall expect you to be my guest."

This settled the embarrassing question which had suggested itself as to where he should stay. His late father's house was of course shut up, and he had no relatives in Willoughby.

"Thank you, Mr. Shaw," he said. "For a few days I shall be glad to accept your kind offer. What progress have you made in settling the estate?"

"I can give you some idea of how it stands. There will be something left, but not much. After paying all debts, including Nancy's, there will certainly be a thousand dollars; but if you pay Nancy's legacy, that will take half of this sum."

"The legacy shall be paid," said Walter, promptly, "no matter how little remains. I am glad there is enough for that."

"I honor your determination, Walter, but I don't think Nancy will be willing to take half of what you have left."

"Then don't let her know how little it is."

"There is a chance of something more. I have made no account of the Great Metropolitan Mining stock, of which your father held shares to the amount of one hundred thousand dollars, cost price. How these will come out is very uncertain, but I think we can get something. Suppose it were only five per cent., that would make five thousand dollars. But it isn't best to count on that."

"I shan't make any account of the mining stock," said Walter. "If I get anything, it will be so much more than I expect."

"That is the best way. It will prevent disappointment."

"How long before we find out about it?"

"It is wholly uncertain. It may be six months; It may be two years. All I can say is, that I will look after your interests."

"Thank you, I am sure of that."

"Now, as to your plans. You were at the Essex Classical Institute, I think?"

"Yes, sir."

"What do you say to going back for a year? It is not an expensive school. You could stay a year, including all expenses, for the sum of five hundred dollars."

Walter shook his head.

"It would consume all my money; and as long as I am not going to college, my present education will be sufficient."

"As to consuming all your money," said Mr. Shaw, "let me say one thing. I received many favors from your father, especially when a young man just starting in business. Let me repay them by paying half your expenses for the next year at school."

"You are very kind, Mr. Shaw," said Walter, gratefully, "and I would accept that favor from you sooner than from any one; but I've made up my mind to take care of myself, *and paddle my own canoe.*"

"Well, perhaps you're right," said the lawyer, kindly; "but at least you will accept my advice. Have you formed any plans for the future?"

CHAPTER XXII. MESSRS. FLINT AND PUSHER.

Now that he was again in his native village, Walter realized how unpleasant had been his position at Mr. Drummond's from the new elasticity and cheerfulness which he felt. There had been something gloomy and oppressive in the atmosphere of his temporary home at Stapleton, and he certainly had very little enjoyment in Joshua's society. Mrs. Drummond was the only one for whom he felt the least regard.

He passed a few days quietly, renewing old acquaintances and friendships. Nancy Forbes had gone to live with a brother, who was an old bachelor, and very glad to have her with him. Her savings and the legacy left her by Mr. Conrad together amounted to a thousand dollars, or rather more,—sufficient to make Nancy rich, in her own opinion. But she was not quite satisfied about the legacy.

"They say, Walter, that you'll be left poor," she said. "You'll need this money."

"No, I shan't, Nancy," answered Walter. "Besides, there's a lot of mining stock that'll come to something,—I don't know how much."

"But I don't feel right about taking this money, Walter."

"You needn't feel any scruples, Nancy. I can take care of myself. I can paddle my own canoe."

"But you haven't got any canoe," said Nancy, who did not comprehend the allusion. "Besides, I don't see how that would help you to a living."

Walter laughed.

"I shall get a canoe, then," he said, "and I'll steer it on to Fortune."

"At any rate," said Nancy, "I will leave you my money when I die."

"Who knows but you'll marry and have a lot of children?"

"That isn't very likely, Walter, and me forty-seven a'ready. I'm most an old woman."

So the conversation ended. Nancy agreed, though reluctantly, to take the legacy, resolved some time or other to leave it to Walter. If she had known how little he really had left, she would not have consented to accept it at all.

The same evening Walter sat in the lawyer's comfortable sitting-room, and together they discussed the future.

"So you want to be a book agent, Walter?" said Mr. Shaw. "I can't say I think very highly of this plan."

"Why not, Mr. Shaw?"

"It will lead to nothing."

"I don't mean to spend my life at it. I am more ambitious than that. But it will give me a chance to travel without expense, and I always wanted to see something of the world."

"How old are you now?"

"Fifteen."

"You are well-grown of your age. You might readily be taken for sixteen."

"Do you really think so?" asked Walter, gratified, like most boys of his age, at being thought to look older than he really was.

"Yes; at sixteen I was smaller than you now are."

"You see, Mr. Shaw, that, as I am so young, even if I spend a year at this business, I shall not be too old to undertake something else afterwards. In the mean time I shall see something of the world."

"Well, Walter, I won't oppose you. If I had not so much confidence in you, I should warn you of the temptations that are likely to beset your youth, left, as you will be, entirely to yourself. Of course you will be thrown among all kinds of associates."

"Yes, sir; but I think I shall be wise enough to avoid what

will do me no good."

"So I hope and believe. Now, what is the name of this publisher you were speaking of?"

"Pusher. He's of the firm of Flint & Pusher."

"I have heard of them. They are an enterprising firm."

"I think I had better start pretty soon, Mr. Shaw. I shall enjoy myself better when I am at work."

"Next Monday, then, if you desire it."

It was then Friday.

On Monday morning Mr. Shaw handed Walter a pocket-book containing a roll of bills. "You will need some money to defray your expenses," he said, "until you are able to earn something. You will find fifty dollars in this pocket-book. There is no occasion to thank me, for I have only advanced it from money realized from your father's estate. If you need any more, you can write me, and I can send you a check or money-order."

"This will be quite enough, Mr. Shaw," said Walter, confidently. "It won't be long before I shall be paying my way; at least I hope so. I don't mean to be idle."

"I am sure you won't be, or you will belie your reputation. Well, good-by, Walter. Write me soon and often. You know I look upon myself as in some sort your guardian."

"I will certainly write you, Mr. Shaw. By the way, I never thought to ask you about the furniture of my room at the Essex Classical Institute."

"It was purchased by the keeper of the boarding-house; at a sacrifice, it is true, but I thought it best to let it go, to save trouble."

Illustration

"I should like to see Lem," thought Walter, with a little sigh as he called to mind the pleasant hours he had passed with his school-fellow. "I'll go back and pay the old institute a visit some time, after I've got back from my travels."

Walter reached New York by ten o'clock. Though his

acquaintance with the city streets was very limited, as he had seldom visited it, he found his way without much trouble to the place of business of Messrs. Flint & Pusher. As they did not undertake to do a retail business, but worked entirely through agents, their rooms were not on the first floor, but on the third. Opening the door of the room, to which he was guided by a directory in the entry beneath, Walter found himself in a large apartment, the floor of which was heaped up with piles of books, chiefly octavos. An elderly gentleman, with a partially bald head, and wearing spectacles, was talking with two men, probably agents.

"Well, young man," said he, in rather a sharp voice, "what can I do for you?"

"Is Mr. Pusher in?" asked Walter.

"He went out for a few minutes; will be back directly. Did you wish particularly to see him?"

"Yes, sir."

"Take a seat, then, and wait till he comes in."

Walter sat down and listened to the conversation.

"You met with fair success, then?" inquired Mr. Flint.

"Yes, the book takes well. I sold ten in one day, and six and eight in other days."

Walter pricked up his ears. He wondered whether the book was the one recommended to him. If so, a sale of ten copies would enable the agent to realize twelve dollars and a half, which was certainly doing very well.

Just as the agents were going out, Mr. Pusher bustled in. His sharp eyes fell upon Walter, whom he immediately recognized.

"Ha, my young friend, so you have found us out," he said, offering his hand.

"Yes, sir."

"Come to talk on business, I hope?"

"Yes, sir, that is my object in coming."

"Mr. Flint," said Mr. Pusher, "this is a young friend whose acquaintance I made a short time since. I told him, if ever he wanted employment, to come here, and we would give him something to do."

Mr. Flint, who was a slower and a more cautious man than Mr. Pusher, regarded Walter a little doubtfully.

"Do you mean as an agent?" he said.

"Certainly I do."

"He seems very young."

"That's true, but age isn't always an advantage. He looks smart, and I'll guarantee that he is all he looks. I claim to be something of a judge of human nature too."

"No doubt you're right," said Mr. Flint, who was accustomed to defer considerably to his more impetuous partner. "What's the young man's name?"

"You've got me there," said Mr. Pusher, laughing. "If I ever knew, which is doubtful, I've forgotten."

"My name is Walter Conrad," said our hero.

"Very good. Well, Conrad," continued Mr. Pusher, in an off-hand manner, "what are your wishes? What book do you want to take hold of?"

"You mentioned a book the other day,—'Scenes in Bible Lands.'"

"Yes, our new book. That would be as good as any to begin on. How's the territory, Mr. Flint?"

Mr. Flint referred to a book.

"Most of the territory near by is taken up," he said. "Does Mr. Conrad wish to operate near home?"

"I would rather go to a distance," said Walter.

"As far as Ohio?"

"Yes."

"In that case you could map out your own route pretty much. We haven't got the West portioned out as we have the

Middle and New England States."

"In other words, we can give you a kind of roving commission, Conrad," put in Mr. Pusher.

"That would suit me, sir," said Walter.

"Still it would be best not to attempt to cover too much territory. A rolling stone gathers no moss, you know. There is one important question I must ask you to begin with. Have you got any money?"

"Yes, sir, I have fifty dollars."

"Good. Of course you will need money to get out to your field of labor, and will have to pay your expenses till you begin to earn something. Fifty dollars will answer very well."

"As I don't know very well how the business is managed," said Walter, "I must ask for instructions."

"Of course. You're a green hand. Sit down here, and I'll make it all plain to you."

So Mr. Pusher, in his brief, incisive way, explained to Walter how he must manage. His instructions were readily comprehended, and Walter, as he listened, felt eager to enter upon the adventurous career which he had chosen.

CHAPTER XXIII. WALTER LOSES HIS MONEY.

Walter, by advice of Mr. Pusher, bought a ticket to Cleveland. There was a resident agent in this city, and a depository of books published by the firm. As Walter would be unable to carry with him as large a supply of books as he needed, he was authorized to send to the Cleveland agency when he got out, and the books would be sent him by express.

"I will give you a letter to Mr. Greene, our agent in Cleveland," said Mr. Pusher, "and you can consult him as to your best field of operations."

The letter was hastily written and handed to Walter.

"Good-by, Mr. Pusher," he said, preparing to leave the office.

"Good-by, my young friend. I shall hope to hear good accounts from you."

So Walter went downstairs, and emerged into the street. He had no particular motive for remaining in New York, and felt eager to commence work. So he went at once to the Erie railway depot, and bought a through ticket to Cleveland, via Buffalo and Niagara Falls. Though he had not much money to spare, he determined not to neglect the opportunity he would have of seeing this great natural wonder, but to stop over a day in order to visit the falls.

He selected a comfortable seat by a window, and waited till the train was ready to start. He realized that he had engaged in rather a large enterprise for a boy of fifteen, who had hitherto had all his wants supplied by others. He was about to go a thousand miles from home, to earn his own living,—in other words, to paddle his own canoe. But he did not feel in the least dismayed. He was ambitious and enterprising, and confident that he could earn his living as well as other boys of his age. He had never been far from home, but felt that he should enjoy visiting new and unfamiliar scenes. So he felt decidedly cheerful and hopeful as the cars whirled him out of the depot, and he commenced his Western journey.

Walter put his strip of railway tickets into his vest-pocket, and his porte-monnaie, containing the balance of his money, into the pocket of his pantaloons. He wished to have the tickets at hand when the conductor came round. He sat alone at first, but after a while a lady got in who rode thirty miles or more, and then got out. A little later a young man passed through the cars, looking about him on either side. He paused at Walter's seat, and inquired, "Is this seat taken?"

"No, sir," said Walter.

"Then, with your permission, I will take it," said the stranger. "Tiresome work travelling, isn't it?"

"I don't know," said Walter. "I rather like it; but then I never travelled much."

"I have to travel a good deal on business," said the other, "and I've got tired of it. How many times do you think I have been over this road?"

"Couldn't guess."

"This is the fifteenth time. I know it like a book. How far are you going?"

"To Cleveland."

"Got relations there, I suppose?"

"No," said Walter; "I am going on business."

He was rather glad to let his companion know that he, too, was in business.

"You're young to be in business," said his companion. "What sort of business is it?"

"I am an agent for Flint & Pusher, a New York firm."

"Publishers, aint they?"

"Yes, sir."

Walter's companion was a young man of twenty-five, or possibly a year or two older. He was rather flashily attired, with a cut-away coat and a low-cut vest, double-breasted, across which glittered a massive chain, which might have been gold, or might only have been gilt, since all that glitters is not gold. At any rate, it answered the purpose of making a show. His cravat was showy, and his whole appearance indicated absence of good taste. A cautious employer would scarcely have selected him from a crowd of applicants for a confidential position. Walter was vaguely conscious of this. Still he had seen but little of the world, and felt incompetent to judge others.

"Are you going right through to Cleveland?" inquired the stranger.

"No; I think I shall stop at Buffalo. I want to see Niagara Falls."

"That's right. Better see them. They're stunning."

"I suppose you have been there?" said Walter, with some curiosity.

"Oh, yes, several times. I've a great mind to go again and show you round, but I don't know if I can spare so long a time from business."

"I should like your company," said Walter, politely; "but I don't want to interfere with your engagements."

"I'll think of it, and see how I can arrange matters," said the other.

Walter was not particularly anxious for the continued society of his present companion. He was willing enough to talk with him, but there was something in his appearance and manner which prevented his being attracted to him. He turned away and began to view the scenery through which they were passing. The stranger took out a newspaper, and appeared to be reading attentively. Half an hour passed thus without a word being spoken on either side. At length his companion folded up the paper.

"Do you smoke?" he asked.

"No," said Walter.

"I think I'll go into the smoking-car, and smoke a cigar. I should like to offer you one if you will take one."

"No, thank you," said Walter; "I don't smoke, and I am afraid my first cigar wouldn't give me much pleasure."

"I'll be back in a few minutes. Perhaps you'd like to look over this paper while I am gone."

"Thank you," said Walter.

He took the paper,—an illustrated weekly,—and looked over the pictures with considerable interest. He had just commenced reading a story when a boy passed through the car with a basket of oranges and apples depending from his arm.

"Oranges—apples!" he called out, looking to the right and left in quest of customers.

The day was warm, and through the open window dust had blown into the car. Walter's throat felt parched, and the oranges looked tempting.

"How much are your oranges?" he inquired.

"Five cents apiece, or three for a dime," answered the boy.

"I'll take three," said Walter, reflecting that he could easily dispose of two himself, and considering that it would only be polite to offer one to his companion, whose paper he was reading, when he should return.

"Here are three nice ones," said the boy, picking them out, and placing them in our hero's hands.

Walter felt in his vest-pocket, thinking he had a little change there. He proved to be mistaken. There was nothing in that pocket except his railway tickets.

Next, of course, he felt for his porte-monnaie, but he felt for it in vain.

He started in surprise.

"I thought my pocket-book was in that pocket," he reflected. "Can it be in the other?"

He felt in the other pocket, but search here was equally fruitless. He next felt nervously in the pocket of his coat, though he was sure he couldn't have put his porte-monnaie there. Then it flashed upon him, with a feeling of dismay, that he had lost his pocket-book and all his remaining money. How or where, he could not possibly imagine, for the suddenness of the discovery quite bewildered him.

"I won't take the oranges," he said to the boy. "I can't find my money."

The boy, who had made sure of a sale, took back the fruit reluctantly, and passed on, crying out, "Here's your oranges and apples!"

Walter set about thinking what had become of his money. The more he thought, the more certain he felt that he had put his porte-monnaie in the pocket in which he had first felt for it. Why was it not there now? That was a question which he felt utterly incompetent to answer.

"Have you lost anything?" inquired a gentleman who sat just behind Walter. Looking back, he found that it was a gentleman of fifty who addressed him.

"Yes, sir," he said, "I have lost my pocket-book."

"Was there much money in it?"

"About forty dollars, sir."

"That is too much to lose. Was your ticket in it also?"

"No, sir; that I have in my vest-pocket."

"Where was your pocket-book when you last saw it?" inquired the gentleman.

"In this pocket, sir."

"Humph!" commented the other. "Who was that young man who was sitting with you a few minutes since?"

"I don't know, sir."

"He was a stranger, then?"

"Yes, sir; I never met him till this morning."

"Then I think I can tell you where your money has

gone."

"Where, sir?" demanded Walter, beginning to understand him.

"I think your late companion was a pickpocket, and relieved you of it, while he pretended to be reading. I didn't like his appearance much."

"I don't see how he could have done it without my feeling his hand in my pocket."

"They understand their business, and can easily relieve one of his purse undetected. I once had my watch stolen without being conscious of it. Your porte-monnaie was in the pocket towards the man, and you were looking from the window. It was a very simple thing to relieve you of it."

CHAPTER XXIV. SLIPPERY DICK.

It is not natural for a boy of Walter's age to distrust those with whom he becomes acquainted even slightly. This lesson unfortunately is learned later in life. But the words of his fellow-traveller inspired him with conviction. He could think of no other way of accounting for his loss.

He rose from his seat.

"Where are you going?" asked the old gentleman.

"I am going to look for the thief."

"Do you expect to find him?"

"He said he was going into the smoking-car."

"My young friend, I strongly suspect that this was only to blind you. The cars have stopped at two stations since he left his seat, and if he took your money he has doubtless effected his escape."

Walter was rather taken aback by this consideration. It seemed reasonable enough, and, if true, he didn't see how he was going to get back his money.

"I dare say you are right," he said; "but I will go into the smoking-car and see."

"Come back again, and let me know whether you find him."

"Yes, sir."

Walter went through two cars, looking about him on either side, thinking it possible that the thief might have taken his seat in one of them. There was very little chance of this, however. Next he passed into the smoking-car, where, to his joy no less than his surprise, he found the man of whom he was in search playing cards with three other passengers.

He looked up carelessly as Walter approached, but did not betray the slightest confusion or sign of guilt. To let the reader into a secret, he had actually taken Walter's pocket-book, but was too cunning to keep it about him. He had taken out the money, and thrown the porte-monnaie itself from the car platform, taking an opportunity when he thought himself unobserved. As the money consisted of bills, which could not be identified as Walter's, he felt that he was in no danger of detection. He thought that he could afford to be indifferent.

"Did you get tired of waiting?" he asked, addressing our hero.

"That's pretty cool if he took the money," thought Walter.

"May I speak to you a moment?" asked Walter.

"Certainly."

"I mean alone."

"If you'll wait till I have finished the game," said the pickpocket, assuming a look of surprise. "Something private, eh?"

"Yes," said Walter, gravely.

He stood by impatiently while the game went on. He was anxious to find out as soon as possible what had become of his money, and what was the chance of recovering it.

At length the game was finished, and a new one was about to be commenced, when Walter tapped his late companion on the shoulder.

"Oh, you wanted to speak to me, did you?" he said indifferently. "Can't you wait till we have finished this game?"

"No," said Walter, resolutely, "I can't wait. It is a matter of great importance."

"Then, gentlemen, I must beg to be excused for five minutes," said the pickpocket, shrugging his shoulders, as if to express good-natured annoyance. "Now, my young friend, I am at your service."

Walter proceeded to the other end of the car, which chanced to be unoccupied. Now that the moment had come, he hardly knew how to introduce the subject. Suppose that the person he addressed were innocent, it would be rather an awkward matter to charge him with the theft.

"Did you see anything of my pocket-book?" he said, at length.

"Your pocket-book?" returned the pickpocket, arching his brows. "Why, have you lost it?"

"Yes."

"When did you discover its loss?"

"Shortly after you left me," said Walter, significantly.

"Indeed! was there much money in it?"

"Over thirty dollars."

"That is quite a loss. I hope you have some more with you."

"No, it is all I have."

"I'm very sorry indeed. I did not see it. Have you searched on the floor?"

"Yes; but it isn't there."

"That's awkward. Was your ticket in the pocket-book?"

"No, I had that in my vest-pocket."

"That's fortunate. On my honor, I'm sorry for you. I haven't much money with me, but I'll lend you a dollar or two with the greatest of pleasure."

This offer quite bewildered Walter. He felt confident that the other had stolen his money, and now here he was offering to lend him some of it. He did not care to make such a compromise, or to be bought off so cheap; so, though quite penniless, he determined to reject the offer.

"I won't borrow," he said, coldly. "I was hoping you had seen my money."

"Sorry I didn't. Better let me lend you some."

"I would rather not borrow."

Walter could not for the life of him add "Thank you," feeling no gratitude to the man who he felt well assured had robbed him.

The pickpocket turned and went back to his game, and Walter slowly left the car. He had intended to ask him point-blank whether he had taken the money, but couldn't summon the necessary courage. He went back to his old seat.

"Well," said the old gentleman who sat behind him, "I suppose you did not find your man?"

"Yes, I did."

"You didn't get your money?" he added, in surprise.

"No, he said he had not seen it."

"Did you tax him with taking it?"

"No, I hardly ventured to do that."

"Did he show any confusion?"

"No, sir, he was perfectly cool. Still, I think he took it. He offered to lend me a dollar or two."

"That was cool, certainly."

"What would you advise me to do?" asked Walter.

"I hardly know what to advise," said the other, thoughtfully.

"I don't want him to make off with my money."

"Of course not. That would be far from agreeable."

"If he could only be searched, I might find the pocket-book on him."

"In order to do that, he must be charged with the robbery."

"That is true. It will be rather awkward for a boy like me to do that."

"I'll tell you what you had better do, my young friend. Speak to the conductor."

"I think I will," said Walter.

Just at that moment the conductor entered the car. As he came up the aisle Walter stopped him, and explained his loss, and the suspicions he had formed.

"You say the man is in the smoking-car?" said the

conductor, who had listened attentively.

"Yes."

"Could you point him out?"

"Yes."

"I am glad of it. I have received warning by telegraph that one of the New York swell-mob is on the train, probably intent on mischief, but no description came with it, and I had no clue to the person. I have no doubt that the man you speak of is the party. If so, he is familiarly known as 'Slippery Dick.'"

"Do you think you can get back my money?" asked Walter, anxiously.

"I think there is a chance of it. Come with me and point out your man."

Walter gladly accompanied the conductor to the smoking-car. His old acquaintance was busily engaged as before in a game, and laughing heartily at some favorable turn.

"There he is," said Walter, indicating him with his finger.

The conductor walked up to him, and tapped him on the shoulder.

"What's wanted?" he asked, looking up. "You've looked at my ticket."

"I wish to speak to you a moment."

He rose without making any opposition, and walked to the other end of the car.

"Well," he said, and there was a slight nervousness in his tone, "what's the matter? Wasn't my ticket all right?"

"No trouble about that. The thing is, will you restore this boy's pocket-book?"

"Sir," said the pickpocket, blustering, "do you mean to insult me? What have I to do with his pocket-book?"

"You sat beside him, and he missed it directly after you left him."

"What is that to me? You may search me if you like. You will find only one pocket-book upon me, and that is my own."

"I am aware of that," said the conductor, coolly. "I saw you take the money out and throw it from the car platform."

The pickpocket turned pale.

"You are mistaken in the person," he said.

"No, I am not. I advise you to restore the money forthwith."

Without a word the thief, finding himself cornered, took from his pocket a roll of bills, which he handed to Walter.

"Is that right?" asked the conductor.

"Yes," said our hero, after counting his money.

"So far, so good. And now, Slippery Dick," he continued, turning to the thief, "I advise you to leave the cars at the next station, or I will have you arrested. Take your choice."

The detected rogue was not long in making his choice. Already the cars had slackened their speed, and a short distance ahead appeared a small station. The place seemed to be one of very little importance. One man, however, appeared to have business there. Walter saw his quondam acquaintance jump on the platform, and congratulated himself that his only loss was a porte-monnaie whose value did not exceed one dollar.

I will only add that the conductor on seeing the pocket-book thrown away had thought nothing of it, supposing it to be an old one, but as soon as he heard of the robbery suspected at once the thief and his motive.

CHAPTER XXV. A HARD CUSTOMER.

Walter stopped long enough at Buffalo to visit Niagara Falls, as he had intended. Though he enjoyed the visit, and found the famous cataract fully up to his expectations, no incident occurred during the visit which deserves to be chronicled here. He resumed his journey, and arrived in due time at Cleveland.

He had no difficulty in finding the office of Mr. Greene, the agent of Messrs. Flint & Pusher. He found that this gentleman, besides his agency, had a book and stationery business of his own.

"I don't go out myself," he said to Walter; "but I keep a supply of Flint's books on hand, and forward them to his agents as called for. Have you done much in the business?"

"No, sir, I am only a beginner. I have done nothing yet."

"I thought not. You look too young."

"Mr. Pusher told me I had better be guided by your advice."

"I'll advise you as well as I can. First, I suppose you want to know where to go."

"Yes, sir."

"You had better go fifty miles off at least. The immediate neighborhood has been pretty well canvassed. There's C—— now, a flourishing and wealthy town. Suppose you go there first."

"Very well, sir."

"It's on the line of railway. Two hours will carry you there."

"I'll go, this afternoon."

"You are prompt."

"I want to get to work as soon as possible."

"I commend your resolution. It speaks well for your success."

Walter arrived in C—— in time for supper. He went to a

small public house, where he found that he could board for a dollar and a half a day, or seven dollars by the week. He engaged a week's board, reflecting that he could probably work to advantage a week in so large a place, or, if not, that five days at the daily rate would amount to more than the weekly terms.

He did not at first propose to do anything that evening until it occurred to him that he might perhaps dispose of a copy of his book to the landlord in part payment for his board. He went into the public room after supper.

"Are you travelling alone?" asked the landlord, who had his share of curiosity.

"Yes," said Walter.

"Not on business?"

"Yes, on business."

"What might it be now? You are rather young to be in business."

"I am a book-agent."

"Meeting with pretty good success?"

"I'm just beginning," said Walter, smiling. "If you'll be my first customer, I'll stop with you a week."

"What kind of a book have you got?"

Walter showed it. It was got up in the usual style of subscription books, with abundance of illustrations.

"It's one of the best books we ever sent out," said Walter, in a professional way. "Just look at the number of pictures. If you've got any children, they'll like it; and, if you haven't, it will be just the book for your centre-table."

"I see you know how to talk," said the landlord, smiling. "What is the price?"

"Three dollars and a half."

"That's considerable."

"But you know I'm going to take it out in board."

"Well, that's a consideration, to be sure. A man doesn't feel it so much as if he took the money out of his pocket and paid cash down. What do you say, Mrs. Burton?" addressing his wife, who just then entered the room. "This young man wants to stay here a week, and pay partly in a book he is agent for. Shall I agree?"

"Let me see the book," said Mrs. Burton, who was a comely, pleasant-looking woman of middle age. "What's the name of it?"

"'Scenes in Bible Lands,'" said Walter.

He opened it, taking care to display and point out the pictures.

"I declare it is a nice book," said Mrs. Burton. "Is there a picture of Jerusalem?"

"Here it is," said Walter, who happened to know just where to find it. "Isn't it a good picture? And there are plenty more as good. It's a book that ought to be in every family."

"Really, Mr. Burton, I don't know but we might as well take it," said the landlady. "He takes it out in board, you know."

"Just as you say," said the landlord. "I am willing."

"Then I'll take the book. Emma will like to look at it."

So Walter made the first sale, on which he realized a profit of one dollar and a quarter.

"It's a pretty easy way to earn money," he reflected with satisfaction, "if I can only sell copies enough. One copy sold will pay for a day's board."

He went to bed early, and enjoyed a sound and refreshing sleep. He was cheered with hopes of success on the morrow. If he could sell four copies a day, that would give him a profit of five dollars, and five dollars would leave him a handsome profit after paying expenses.

The next morning after breakfast he started out, carrying with him three books. Knowing nothing of the residents of the village, he could only judge by the outward appearance of their houses. Seeing a large and handsome house standing back from the street, he decided to call.

"The people living here must be rich," he thought. "They won't mind paying three dollars and a half for a nice book."

Accordingly he walked up the gravelled path and rang the front-door bell. The door was opened by a housemaid.

"Is the lady of the house at home?" asked Walter.

"Do you want to see her?"

"Yes."

"Then wait here, and I'll tell her."

A tall woman, with a thin face and a pinched expression, presented herself after five minutes.

"Well, young man," she asked, after a sharp glance, "what is your business?"

Her expression was not very encouraging, but Walter was bound not to lose an opportunity.

"I should like to show you a new book, madam," he commenced, "a book of great value, beautifully illustrated, which is selling like wildfire."

"How many copies have you sold?" inquired the lady, sharply.

"One," answered Walter, rather confused.

"Do you call that selling like wildfire?" she demanded with sarcasm.

"I only commenced last evening," said Walter, "I referred to the sales of other agents."

"What's the name of the book?"

"'Scenes in Bible Lands.'"

"Let me see it."

Walter displayed the book.

"Look at the beautiful pictures," he said.

"I don't see anything remarkable about them. The binding isn't very strong. Shouldn't wonder if the book would go to pieces in a week."

"I don't think there'll be any trouble that way," said Walter.

"If it does, you'll be gone, so it won't trouble you."

"With ordinary care it will hold long enough."

"Oh, yes, of course you'd say so. I expected it. How much do you charge for the book?"

"Three dollars and a half."

"Three dollars and a half!" repeated the woman. "You seem to think people are made of money."

"I don't fix the price, madam," said Walter, rather provoked. "The publishers do that."

"I warrant they make two-thirds profit. Don't they now?"

"I don't know," said Walter. "I don't know anything about the cost of publishing books; but this is a large one, and there are a great many pictures in it. They must have cost considerable."

"Seems to me it's ridiculous to ask such a price for a book. Why, it's enough to buy a nice dress pattern!"

"The book will last longer than the dress," said Walter.

"But it is not so necessary. I'll tell you what I'll do. I'd like the book well enough to put on my parlor-table. I'll give you two dollars for it."

"Two dollars!" ejaculated Walter, scarcely crediting the testimony of his ears.

"Yes, two dollars; and I warrant you'll make money enough then."

"I should lose money," said Walter. "I couldn't think of accepting such an offer."

"In my opinion there isn't any book worth even two dollars."

"I see we can't trade," said Walter, disgusted at such meanness in a lady who occupied so large a house, and might be supposed to have plenty of money.

He began to replace the book in its brown-paper covering.

"I don't know but I might give you twenty-five cents more. Come now, I'll give you two dollars and a quarter."

"I can't take it," said Walter, shortly. "Three dollars and a half is the price, and I will not take a cent less."

"You won't get it out of me then," retorted the lady, slamming the door in displeasure.

Walter had already made up his mind to this effect, and had started on his way to the gate.

"I wonder if I shall meet many people like her," he thought, and his courage was rather damped.

CHAPTER XXVI. BUSINESS EXPERIENCES.

Walter began to think that selling books would prove a harder and more disagreeable business than he anticipated. He had been brought face to face with meanness and selfishness, and they inspired him with disgust and indignation. Not that he expected everybody to buy his books, even if they could afford it. Still it was not necessary to insult him by offering half price.

He walked slowly up the street, wondering if he should meet any more such customers. On the opposite side of the street he noticed a small shoemaker's shop.

"I suppose it is of no use to go in there," thought Walter. "If they won't buy at a big house, there isn't much chance here."

Still he thought he would go in. He had plenty of time on his hands, and might as well let slip no chance, however small.

He pushed open the door, and found himself in a shop about twenty-five feet square, littered up with leather shavings and finished and unfinished shoes. A boy of fourteen was pegging, and his father, a man of middle age, was finishing a shoe.

"Good-morning," said Walter.

"Good-morning," said the shoemaker, turning round. "Do you want a pair of shoes this morning?"

"No," said Walter, "I didn't come to buy, but to sell."

"Well, what have you got to sell?"

"A subscription book, finely illustrated."

"What's the name of it?"

"'Scenes in Bible Lands.'"

"Let me look at it."

He wiped his hands on his apron, and, taking the book, began to turn over the leaves.

"It seems like a good book," he said. "Does it sell well?"

"Yes, it sells largely. I have only just commenced, but other agents are doing well on it."

"You are rather young for an agent."

"Yes, but I'm old enough to work, and I'm going to give this a fair trial."

"That's the way to talk. How much do you expect to get for this book?"

"The price is three dollars and a half."

"It's rather high."

"But there are a good many pictures. Those are what cost money."

"Yes, I suppose they do. Well, I've a great mind to take one."

"I don't think you'll regret it. A good book will give you pleasure for a long time."

"That's so. Well, here's the money;" and the shoemaker drew out five dollars from a leather pocket-book. "Can you give me the change?"

"With pleasure."

Walter was all the more pleased at effecting this sale because it was unexpected. He had expected to sell a book at the great house he had just called at, but thought that the price of the book might deter the shoemaker, whose income probably was not large. He thought he would like to know the name of the lady with whom he had such an unpleasant experience.

"Can you tell me," he inquired, "who lives in that large house a little way up the street?"

"You didn't sell a book there, did you?" asked the shoemaker, laughing.

"No, but I got an offer of two dollars for one."

"That's just like Mrs. Belknap," returned the other. "She has the name of being the meanest woman for miles around."

"It can't be for want of money. She lives in a nice house."

"Oh, she's rich enough,—the richest woman in town. When her husband was alive—old Squire Belknap—she wasn't quite so scrimping, for he was free-handed and liberal himself; but now she's a widow, she shows out her meanness. So she offered you two dollars?"

"Yes, but she afterwards offered twenty-five cents more."

"Then she must have wanted the book. She makes it her boast that no peddler ever took her in, and I guess she's about right."

"I hope there are not many such people in town. If there are, I shall get discouraged."

"We've got our share of mean people, I expect, but she's the worst."

"Well, I suppose I must be going. Thank you for your purchase."

"That's all right. If I like the book as well as I expect, I'll thank you."

Walter left the shoemaker's shop with considerably higher spirits than he entered. His confidence in human nature, which had been rudely shaken by Mrs. Belknap, was in a degree restored, and his prospects looked brighter than a few minutes before.

"I wonder who'll make the next purchase?" he thought.

He stopped at a plain two-story house a little further up the road. The door was opened by an old lady.

"What do you want?" she asked.

"I am agent for an excellent book," commenced Walter.

"Oh, you're a peddler," broke in the old lady, without waiting to hear him through.

"I suppose I may be called so."

"Are you the man that was round last spring selling jewelry?"

"No, I have never been here before."

"I don't know whether to believe you or not," said the old lady. "Your voice sounds like his. I can't see very well, for I've mislaid my specs. If you're the same man, I'll have you took up for selling bogus jewelry."

"But I'm not the same one."

"I don't know. The man I spoke of sold my darter a gold ring for a dollar, that turned out to be nothing but brass washed over. 'Twa'n't worth five cents."

"I'm sorry you got cheated, but it isn't my fault."

"Wait a minute, I'll call my darter."

In reply to her mother's call a tall maiden lady of forty advanced to the door, with some straw in her hand, for she was braiding straw.

"What's wanted, mother?" she asked.

"Isn't this the same man that sold you that ring?"

"La, no, mother. He was a man of forty-five, and this is only a boy."

"I s'pose you must be right, but I can't see without my specs. Well, I'm sorry you're not the one, for I'd have had you took up onless you'd give back the dollar."

Under the circumstances Walter himself was not sorry that there was no chance of identifying him with his knavish predecessor.

"What have you got to sell?" asked the younger woman.

"A book beautifully illustrated, called 'Scenes in Bible Lands.' Will you allow me to show it to you?"

"He seems quite polite," said the old lady, now disposed to regard Walter more favorably. "Won't you come in?"

Walter entered, and was shown into a small sitting-room, quite plainly furnished. The book was taken from him, and examined for a considerable length of time by the daughter, who, however, announced at the end that though she should like it very much, she couldn't afford to pay the price. As the appearance of the house bore out her assertion, Walter did not press the purchase, but was about to replace the book under his arm, when she said suddenly, "Wait a minute. There's Mrs. Thurman just coming in. Perhaps she'll buy one of your books."

Walter was of course perfectly willing to wait on the

chance of a sale.

Mrs. Thurman was the wife of a trader in good circumstances, and disposed to spend liberally, according to her means. Walter was not obliged to recommend his book, for this was done by the spinster, who was disinterestedly bent on making a sale. So he sat quiet, a passive but interested auditor, while Miss Nancy Sprague extolled the book for him.

"It does seem like an excellent book," said Mrs. Thurman, looking at the pictures.

"Just the thing for your Delia," suggested Miss Nancy; "I am sure she would like it."

"That reminds me to-morrow is Delia's birthday."

"Then give her the book for a birthday present."

"I had intended to buy her something else. Still I am not sure but this would suit her quite as well."

"I am sure it would," responded Miss Nancy.

"Then I will take it. Young man, how much do you ask for your book?"

"Three dollars and a half."

Mrs. Thurman paid the money, and received the book.

"I am much obliged to you," said Walter, addressing Miss Nancy, "for recommending my book."

"You're quite welcome," said Miss Nancy, who felt some satisfaction at gaining her point, though it would not benefit her any. "I'm sure you are quite polite for a peddler, and I hope you'll excuse mother for making such a mistake about you."

"That is of no consequence," said Walter, smiling. "I think if your mother had had her glasses on she would not have made such a mistake."

He left the house still farther encouraged. But during the next hour he failed to sell another copy. At length he managed to sell a third. As these were all he had brought out, and he was feeling rather tired, he went back to the tavern, and did not come out again till after dinner. He had sold three copies and cleared three dollars and seventy-five cents, which he was right in regarding as very fair success.

CHAPTER XXVII. A CABIN IN THE WOODS.

Walter found a good dinner ready for him at twelve o'clock, which he enjoyed the more because he felt that he had earned it in advance. He waited till about two o'clock, and again set out, this time in a different direction. As it takes all sorts of people to make a world, so the reception he met with at different places differed. In some he was received politely; in others he was treated as a humbug. But Walter was by this time getting accustomed to his position, and found that he must meet disagreeable people with as good humor as he could command. One farmer was willing to take the book if he would accept pay in apples, of which he offered him two barrels; but this offer he did not for a moment entertain, judging that he would find it difficult to carry about the apples, and probably difficult to dispose of them. However, he managed to sell two copies, though he had to call at twenty places to do it. Nevertheless, he felt well repaid by the degree of success he met with.

"Five books sold to-day!" thought Walter, complacently, as he started on his walk home. "That gives me six dollars and a quarter profit. I wish I could keep that up."

But our young merchant found that he was not likely to keep up such sales. The next day he sold but two copies, and the day succeeding three. Still for three days and a half the aggregate sale was eleven copies, making a clear profit of thirteen dollars and seventy-five cents. At the end of the week he had sold twenty copies; but to make up this number he had been obliged to visit one or two neighboring villages.

He now prepared to move on. The next place at which he proposed to stop for a few days we will call Bolton. He had already written to Cleveland for a fresh supply of books to be forwarded to him there. He had but two books left, and his baggage being contained in a small valise, he decided to walk this distance, partly out of economy, but principally because it would enable him to see the country at his leisure. During the first five miles he succeeded in selling both books, which relieved him of the burden of carrying them, leaving him only his valise.

Walter was strong and stout, and enjoyed his walk. There was a freshness and novelty about his present mode of life, which he liked. He did not imagine he should like to be a book-agent all his life, but for a time he found it quite agreeable.

He stopped under the shade of a large elm and ate the lunch which he had brought with him from the inn. The sandwiches and apples were good, and, with the addition of some water from a stream near by, made a very acceptable lunch. When he resumed his walk after resting a couple of hours, the weather had changed. In the morning it was bright sunshine. Now the clouds had gathered, and a storm seemed imminent. To make matters worse, Walter had managed to stray from the road. He found himself walking in a narrow lane, lined on either side by thick woods. Soon the rain come pattering down, at first in small drops, but quickly poured down in a drenching shower. Walter took refuge in the woods, congratulating himself that he had sold the books, which otherwise would have run the risk of being spoiled.

"I wish there were some house near by in which I could rest," thought Walter. The prospect of being benighted in the woods in such weather was far from pleasant.

Looking around anxiously, he espied a small foot-path, which he followed, hoping, but hardly expecting, that it might lead to some place of refuge. To his agreeable surprise he emerged after a few minutes into a small clearing, perhaps half an acre in extent, in the middle of which was a rough cabin. It was a strange place for a house, but, rude as it was, Walter hailed its appearance with joy. At all events it promised protection from the weather, and the people who occupied it would doubtless be willing to give him, for pay of course, supper and lodging. Probably the accommodations would not be first class, but our hero was prepared to take what he could get, and be thankful for it. Accordingly he advanced fearlessly and pounded on the door with his fist, as there was neither bell nor knocker.

The door not being opened immediately, he pounded again. This time a not particularly musical voice was heard from within:—

"Is that you, Jack?"

"No," answered Walter, "it isn't Jack."

His voice was probably recognized as that of a boy, and any apprehension that might have been felt by the person within was dissipated. Walter heard a bolt withdrawn, and the door opening revealed a tall, gaunt, bony woman, who eyed him in a manner which could not be considered very friendly or cordial.

"Who are you?" she demanded abruptly, keeping the door partly closed.

"I am a book-agent," said Walter.

"Do you expect to sell any books here?" asked the woman, with grim humor.

"No," said Walter, "but I have been caught in the storm, and lost my way. Can I stop here over night if the storm should hold on?"

"This isn't a tavern," said the woman, ungraciously.

"No, I suppose not," said Walter; "but it will be a favor to me if you will take me in, and I will pay you whatever you think right. I suppose there is no tavern near by."

He half hoped there might be, for he had already made up his mind that this would not be a very agreeable place to stop at.

"There's one five miles off," said the woman.

"That's too far to go in such weather. If you'll let me stay here, I will pay you whatever you ask in advance."

"Humph!" said the woman, doubtfully, "I don't know how Jack will like it."

As Walter could know nothing of the sentiments of the Jack referred to, he remained silent, and waited for the woman to make up her mind, believing that she would decide in his favor.

He proved to be right.

"Well," she said, half unwillingly, "I don't know but I'll take you in, though it isn't my custom to accommodate travellers."

"I will try not to give you much trouble," said Walter, relieved to find that he was sure of food and shelter.

"Humph!" responded the woman.

She led the way into the building, which appeared to contain two rooms on the first floor, and probably the same number of chambers above. There was no entry, but the door opened at once into the kitchen.

"Come up to the fire if you're wet," said the woman.

The invitation was hospitable, but the manner was not. However, Walter was glad to accept the invitation, without thinking too much of the manner in which it was expressed, for his clothes were pretty well saturated by the rain. There was no stove, but an old brick fireplace, on which two stout logs were burning. There was one convenience at least about living in the woods. Fuel was abundant, and required nothing but the labor of cutting it.

"I think I'll take off my shoes," said Walter.

"You can if you want to," said his grim hostess.

He extended his wet feet towards the fire, and felt a sense of comfort stealing over him. He could hear the rain falling fiercely against the sides of the cabin, and felt glad that he was not compelled to stand the brunt of the storm.

He looked around him guardedly, not wishing to let his hostess see that he was doing so, for she looked like one who might easily be offended. The room seemed remarkably bare of furniture. There was an unpainted table, and there were also three chairs, one of which had lost its back. These were plain wooden chairs, and though they appeared once to have been painted, few vestiges of the original paint now remained. On a shelf were a few articles of tin, but no articles of crockery were visible, except two cracked cups. Walter had before this visited the dwellings of the poor, but he had never seen a home so poorly provided with what are generally regarded as the necessaries of life.

"I wonder what Lem would say if he should see me now," thought Walter, his thoughts going back to the Essex Classical Institute, and the friend whose studies he shared. They seemed far away, those days of careless happiness, when as yet the burdens of life were unfelt and scarcely even dreamed of. Did Walter sigh for their return? I think not, except on one account. His father was then alive, and he would have given years of his own life to recall that loved parent from the grave. But I do not think he would have cared, for the present at least, to give up his business career, humble though it was, and go back to his studies. He enjoyed the novelty of his position. He enjoyed even his present adventure, in spite of the discomforts that attended it, and there was something exciting in looking about him, and realizing that he was a guest in a rough cabin in the midst of the woods, a thousand miles away from home.

Guarded as he had been in looking around him, it did not escape without observation.

"Well, young man, this is a poor place, isn't it?" asked the woman, suddenly.

"I don't know," said Walter, wishing to be polite.

"That's what you're thinkin', I'll warrant," said the woman. "Well, you're not obliged to stay, if you don't want to."

"But I do want to, and I am very much obliged to you for consenting to take me," said Walter, hastily.

"You said you would pay in advance," said the woman.

"So I will," said Walter, taking out his pocket-book, "if you will tell me how much I am to pay."

"You may give me a dollar," said the woman.

Walter drew out a roll of bills, and, finding a one-dollar note, handed it to the woman.

She took it, glancing covetously at the remaining money which he replaced in his pocket-book. Walter noticed the glance, and, though he was not inclined to be suspicious, it gave him a vague feeling of anxiety.

CHAPTER XXVIII. STRANGE ACQUAINTANCES.

An hour passed without a word being spoken by his singular hostess. She went to the window from time to time, and looked out as if expecting some one. At length Walter determined to break the silence, which had become oppressive. It did not seem natural for two persons to be in the same room so long without speaking a word.

"I should think you would find it lonely living in the woods away from any neighbors," he said.

"I don't care for neighbors," said the woman, shortly.

"Have you lived here long?"

"That's as people reckon time," was the answer.

Walter found himself no wiser than before, and the manner of his hostess did not encourage him to pursue his inquiries further on that subject.

"You don't have far to go for fuel," was the next remark of our hero.

"Any fool might see that," said the woman.

"Not very polite," thought Walter.

He relapsed into silence, judging that his hostess did not care to converse. Soon, however, she began to ask questions.

"Did you say you was a book-peddler?" she inquired.

"I am a book-agent."

"Where are your books,—in that carpet-bag?"

"No, I have sold all my books, and sent for some more."

"Where did you sell them?"

"In C——."

"Have you come from there?"

"Yes, I started from there this forenoon."

"Where did you stop?"

"At the tavern."

"Is your business a good one?" she asked, eying him attentively.

"I have done very well so far, but then I have been at it only a week."

"It's a good thing to have money," said the woman, more to herself than to Walter.

"Yes," said Walter, "it's very convenient to have money; but there are other things that are better."

"Such as what?" demanded the woman abruptly.

"Good health for one thing."

"What else?"

"A good conscience."

She laughed scornfully.

"I'll tell you there's nothing so good as money. I've wanted it all my life, and never could get it. Do you think I would live here in the woods if I had money? No, I should like to be a lady, and wear fine clothes, and drive about in a handsome carriage. Why are some people so lucky, while I live in this miserable hole?"

She looked at Walter fiercely, as if she held him responsible for her ill-fortune.

"Perhaps your luck will change some day," he said, though he had little faith in his own words. He wondered how the tall, gaunt woman of the backwoods would look dressed in silks and satins.

"My luck never will change," she said, quickly.

"I must live and die in some such hovel as this."

"My luck has changed," said Walter, quietly; "but in a different way."

"How?" she asked, betraying in her tone some curiosity.

"A year ago—six months ago—my father was a rich man, or was considered so. He was thought to be worth over a hundred thousand dollars. All at once his property was swept away, and now I am obliged to earn my own living, as you see."

"Is that true?" she asked.

"Yes, it is true."

"How did your father lose his money?"

"By speculating in mines."

"The more fool he!"

"My father is dead," said Walter, gravely. "I cannot bear to hear him blamed."

"Humph!" ejaculated the woman; but what she intended to convey by this utterance Walter could not tell.

Again the woman went to the window and looked out.

"It's time for Jack to be here," she said.

"Your son?" asked Walter.

"No, my husband."

"He'll be pretty wet when he comes in," Walter ventured to say; but his remark elicited no response.

After a while his hostess said, in her usual abrupt tone, "I expect you are hungry."

"Yes," said Walter, "I am, but I can wait till your husband comes."

"I don't know when he'll come. Likely he's kept."

She took out from a small cupboard a plate of bread and some cold meat, and laid them on the table. Then she steeped some tea, and, when it was ready, she put that also on the table.

"Set up," she said, briefly.

Walter understood from this that supper was ready, and, putting on his shoes, which were now dry, he moved his chair up.

"Likely you're used to something better," said the woman.

This was true, but our hero politely said that the supper looked very good, and he did not doubt he would enjoy it.

"That's lucky, for it's all you will get," said the woman.

"There's not much use in wasting politeness on her," thought Walter. "She won't give any in return, that's certain."

The woman poured him out some tea in one of the cracked cups.

"We haven't got no milk nor sugar," she said. "My man and I don't care for them."

The first sip of the tea, which was quite strong, nearly caused a wry expression on Walter's face, but he managed to control himself so far as not to betray his want of relish for the beverage his hostess offered him. The only redeeming quality it had was that it was hot, and, exposed as he had been to the storm, warm drink was agreeable.

"There's some bread and there's some meat," said the woman. "You can help yourself."

"Are you not going to eat supper with me?" asked Walter.

"No, I shall wait for Jack."

She sat down in a chair before the fire, leaving Walter to take care of himself, and seemed plunged in thought.

"What a strange woman!" thought Walter. "I wonder if her husband is anything like her. If he is, they must be an agreeable couple."

He ate heartily of the food, and succeeded in emptying his cup of tea. He would have taken another cup if there had been milk and sugar, but it was too bitter to be inviting.

"Will you have some more tea?" asked the hostess, turning round.

"No, I thank you."

"You miss the milk and sugar?"

"I like them in tea."

"We can't afford to buy them, so it's lucky we don't like them."

There was a bitterness in her tone whenever she talked of money, which led Walter to avoid the topic. Evidently she was a discontented woman, angry because her lot in life was not brighter.

Walter pushed his chair from the table, and sat down again before the fire. She rose and cleared the table, replacing the bread and meat in the cupboard.

"Where are you going next?" she asked, after a pause.

Walter mentioned the name of the place.

"Have you ever been there?" he asked.

"Yes."

"Is it a flourishing place?"

"Yes, good enough, but I haven't been there for a year. It may have burned down for all I know."

"I wonder what sort of a woman she was when she was young?" thought Walter. "I wonder if she was always so unsociable?"

There was silence for another hour. Walter wished it were time to go to bed, for the presence of such a woman made him feel uncomfortable. But it was too early yet to suggest retiring.

At length the silence was broken by a step outside.

"That's Jack," said the woman, rising hastily; and over her face there came a transient gleam of satisfaction, the first Walter had observed.

Before she could reach the door it was opened, and Jack entered. Walter looked up with some curiosity to see what sort of a man the husband of this woman might be. He saw a stout man, with a face like a bull-dog's, lowering eyes, and matted red hair and beard.

"They are fitly mated," thought our hero.

The man stopped short as his glance rested upon Walter, and he turned quickly to his wife.

"Who have you got here, Meg?" he asked, in a rough voice.

"He was overtaken by the storm, and wanted me to take him in, and give him supper and lodging."

"He's a boy. What brings him into these woods?"

"He says he's a book-peddler."

"Where are his books?"

"I have sold them all," said Walter, feeling called upon to take a personal share in the conversation.

"How many did you have?"

"Twenty."

"How much did you charge for them?"

"Three dollars and a half apiece."

"That's seventy dollars, isn't it?"

"Yes."

"Well, you can stay here all night if you want to. We aint used to keepin' a tavern, but you'll fare as well as we."

"Thank you. I was afraid I might have to stay out all night."

"Now, Meg, get me something to eat quick. I'm most famished."

While his wife was getting out the supper again, he sat down beside the fire, and Walter had a chance to scan his rough features. There was something in his appearance that inspired distrust, and our hero wished the night were past, and he were again on his way.

CHAPTER XXIX. DANGER THREATENS.

After supper, which the man devoured like a wild animal, he proved more sociable. He tried in a rough, uncouth manner to make himself agreeable, and asked Walter numerous questions.

"Do you like peddlin'?" he asked.

"I can't tell yet," said Walter. "I haven't been at it long enough."

"You can make money pretty fast?"

"I don't know. Some days I expect to do well, but other days I may not sell any books. But I like travelling about from place to place."

"I don't know but I should like travellin' myself," said Jack. "Hey, Meg?"

"Anything better than staying in this miserable hole," said the woman. "I'm sick and tired of it."

"Well, old woman, maybe we'll start off soon. You couldn't get me a chance in your business, could you?"

Walter doubted strongly whether a rough, uneducated man like the one before him would be well adapted for the book business, but he did not venture to say so.

"If you would like to try it," he said, "I can give you the name of the agent in Cleveland. He is authorized to employ agents, and might engage you."

"Would he engage the old woman too?"

"I don't know whether he has any female agents."

"I couldn't do nothing sellin' books," said Meg, "nor you either. If it was something else, I might make out."

"Well, we'll think about it. This aint a very cheerful place to live, as you say, and it's about time for a change."

About nine o'clock Walter intimated a desire to go to bed.

"I have been walking considerable to-day," he said, "and I feel tired."

"I'll show you the place you're to sleep in," said the

woman.

She lit a candle, and left the room, followed by Walter. She led the way up a rough, unpainted staircase and opened the door of the room over the one in which they had been seated.

"We don't keep a hotel," said she, "and you must shift as well as you can. We didn't ask you to stay."

Looking around him, Walter found that the chamber which he had entered was as bare as the room below, if not more so. There was not even a bedstead, but in the corner there was a bed on the floor with some ragged bedclothes spread over it.

"That's where you're to sleep," said the woman, pointing it out.

"Thank you," said Walter.

"There isn't much to thank me for. Good-night."

"Good-night," said Walter.

She put the candle on the mantel-piece, for there was no bureau or table in the room, and went out.

"This isn't a very stylish tavern, that's a fact," thought Walter, taking a survey of the room. "I shall have a hard bed, but I guess I can stand it for one night."

There was something else that troubled him more than the poor accommodations. The ill looks of his host and hostess had made a strong impression upon his mind. The particular inquiries which they had made about his success in selling books, and their strong desire for money, led him to feel apprehensive of robbery. He was in the heart of the woods, far away from assistance, and at their mercy. What could he, a boy of fifteen, do against their combined attack? He would have preferred to sleep in the woods without a shelter, rather than have placed himself in their power.

Under the influence of this apprehension, he examined the door to see if there was any way of locking it. But there was neither lock nor bolt. There had been a bolt once, but there was none now.

Next he looked about the room to see if there was any heavy article of furniture with which he could barricade the door. But, as has already been said, there was neither bureau nor table. In fact, there was absolutely no article of furniture except a single wooden chair, and that, of course, would be of no service.

"What shall I do?" thought Walter. "That man can enter the room when I am asleep, and rob me of all my money."

It was a perplexing position to be in, and might have puzzled an older and more experienced traveller than our young hero. He opened his pocket-book, and, taking out the money, counted it. There were sixty dollars and a few cents within.

"Where shall I hide it?" he considered.

Looking about the room, he noticed a closet, the door of which was bolted on the outside. Withdrawing the bolt he opened the door and looked in. It was nearly empty, containing only a few articles of little or no value. A plan of operations rapidly suggested itself to Walter in case the room should be entered while he was awake. In pursuance of this plan he threw a few pennies upon the floor of the closet, and then closed the door again. Next he drew from the pocket-book all the money it contained, except a single five-dollar bill. The bank notes thus removed amounted to fifty-five dollars. He then drew off his stockings, and, laying the bills in the bottom, again put them on.

"He won't suspect where they are," thought Walter, in a tone of satisfaction. "If he takes my pocket-book, I can stand the loss of five dollars."

He put on his shoes, that he might be ready for instant flight, if occasion required it, and threw himself down on the outside of the coverlid.

If our young hero, who, I hope, will prove such if the danger which he fears actually comes, could have overheard the conversation which was even then going on between Jack and Meg, he would have felt that his apprehensions were not without cause.

When the woman returned from conducting Walter to his room, she found her husband sitting moodily beside the fire.

"Well, Meg," he said, looking up, "where did you put him?"

"In the room above."

"I hope he'll sleep sound," said Jack, with a sinister smile. "I'll go up by and by and see how he rests."

"What do you mean to do?" asked Meg.

"He has got seventy dollars in that pocket-book of his. It must be ours."

His wife did not answer immediately, but looked thoughtfully into the fire.

"Well, what do you say?" he demanded impatiently.

"What do I say? That I have no objection to taking the money, if there is no danger."

"What danger is there?"

"He may charge us with the theft."

"He can't see me take it, when his eyes are shut."

"But he may not be asleep."

"So much the worse for him. I must have the money. Seventy dollars is worth taking, Meg. It's more money than I've had in my hands at one time for years."

"I like money as well as you, Jack; but the boy will make a fuss when he finds the money is gone."

"So much the worse for him," said Jack, fiercely. "I'll stop his noise very quick."

"You won't harm the lad, Jack?" said Meg, earnestly.

"Why not? What is he to you?"

"Nothing, but I feel an interest in him. I don't want him harmed. Rob him if you will, but don't hurt him."

"What should you care about him? You never saw him before to-day."

"He told me his story. He has had ill-luck, like us. His father was very rich, not long since, but he suddenly lost all his property, and this boy is obliged to go out as a book-peddler."

"What has that to do with us?"

"You mustn't harm him, Jack."

"I suppose you would like to have him inform against us, and set the police on our track."

"No, I wouldn't, and you know it."

"Then he must never leave this cabin alive," said Jack.

"You would not murder him?" demanded Meg, horror-struck.

"Yes, I would, if there is need of it."

"Then I will go up and bid him leave the house. Better turn him out into the forest than keep him here for that."

She had got half way to the door when her husband sprang forward, and clutched her fiercely by the shoulder.

"What are you going to do?" he growled.

"You shall not kill him. I will send him away."

"I have a great mind to kill you," he muttered fiercely.

"No, Jack, you wouldn't do that. I'm not a very good woman, but I've been a faithful wife to you, and you wouldn't have the heart to kill me."

"How do you know?" he said.

"I know you wouldn't. I am not afraid for myself, but for you as well as this boy. If you killed him, you might be hung, and then what would become of me?"

"What else can I do?" asked her husband, irresolutely.

"Threaten him as much as you like. Make him take an oath never to inform against you. He's a boy that'll keep his oath."

"What makes you think so?"

"I read it in his face. It is an honest face, and it can be trusted."

"Well, old woman, perhaps you are right. The other way is dangerous, and if this will work as well, I don't mind trying it. Now let us go to bed, and when the boy's had time to fall asleep, I'll go in and secure the money."

CHAPTER XXX. THE ROBBER WALKS INTO A TRAP.

Walter's feelings, as he lay on his hard bed on the floor, were far from pleasant. He was not sure that an attempt would be made to rob him, but the probability seemed so great that he could not compose himself to sleep. Suspense was so painful that he almost wished that Jack would come up if he intended to. He was tired, but his mental anxiety triumphed over his bodily fatigue, and he tossed about restlessly.

It was about nine o'clock when he went to bed. Two hours passed, and still there were no signs of the apprehended invasion.

But, five minutes later, a heavy step was heard upon the staircase, which creaked beneath the weight of the man ascending. Jack tried to come up softly, but it creaked nevertheless.

Walter's heart beat quick, as he heard the steps approaching nearer and nearer. It was certainly a trying moment, that might have tested the courage of one older than our hero. Presently the door opened softly, and Jack advanced stealthily into the chamber, carrying a candle which, however, was unlighted. He reckoned upon finding Walter undressed, and his clothes hanging over the chair; but the faint light that entered through the window showed him that his intended victim had not removed his clothing. Of course this made the task of taking his pocket-book much more difficult.

"Confusion!" he muttered. "The boy hasn't undressed."

Walter had closed his eyes, thinking it best to appear to be asleep; but he heard this exclamation, and it satisfied him of Jack's dishonest intentions.

The robber paused a moment, and then, stooping over, inserted his hand into Walter's pocket. He drew out the pocket-book, Walter making no sign of being aware of what was going on.

"I've got it," muttered Jack, with satisfaction, and

stealthily retraced his steps to the door. He went out, carefully closing it after him, and again the steps creaked beneath his weight.

"I'm afraid he'll come back when he finds how little there is in it," thought Walter. "If so, I must trust to my plan."

Meg looked up with interest when her husband re-entered the room. She had been listening with nervous interest, fearing that there might be violence done. She had been relieved to hear no noise, and to see her husband returning quietly.

"Have you got the pocket-book?" she asked.

"Yes, Meg," he said, displaying it. "He went to bed with his clothes on, but I pulled it out of his pocket, as he lay asleep, and he will be none the wiser."

"How much is there in it?"

"I'm going to see. I haven't opened it yet."

He opened the pocket-book, and uttered a cry of disappointment.

"That's all," he said, displaying the five-dollar bill. "He must have had more."

"He did have more. When he paid me the dollar for stoppin' here, he took it from a roll of bills."

"What's he done with 'em, the young rascal?"

"Perhaps he had another pocket-book. But that's the one he took out when he paid me."

"I must go up again, Meg. He had seventy dollars, and I'm goin' to have the rest. Five dollars won't pay me for the trouble of stealin' it."

"Don't hurt the boy, Jack."

"I will, if he don't fork over the money," said her husband, fiercely.

There was no longer any thought of concealment. It was necessary to wake Walter to find out where he had put the money. So Jack went upstairs boldly, not trying to soften the noise of his steps now, angry to think that he had been put to this extra trouble. Walter heard him coming, and guessed what brought him back. I will not deny that he felt nervous, but he determined to act manfully, whatever might be the result. He breathed a short prayer to God for help, for he knew that in times of peril he is the only sufficient help.

The door was thrown open, and Jack strode in, bearing in his hand a candle, this time lighted. He advanced to the bed, and, bending over, shook Walter vigorously.

"What's the matter?" asked our hero, this time opening his eyes, and assuming a look of surprise. "Is it time to get up?"

"It's time for you to get up."

"It isn't morning, is it?"

"No; but I've got something to say to you."

"Well," said Walter, sitting up in the bed, "I'm ready."

"Where've you put that money you had last night?"

"Why do you want to know?" demanded Walter, eying his host fixedly.

"No matter why I want to know," said Jack, impatiently. "Tell me, if you know what's best for yourself."

Walter put his hand in his pocket.

"It was in my pocket-book," he said; "but it's gone."

"Here is your pocket-book," said Jack, producing it.

"Did you take it out of my pocket? What made you take it?"

"None of your impudence, boy!"

"Is it impudent to ask what made you take my property?" said Walter, firmly.

"Yes, it is," said Jack, with an oath.

"Do you mean to steal my money?"

"Yes, I do; and the sooner you hand it over the better."

"You have got my pocket-book already."

"Perhaps you think I am green," sneered Jack. "I found

only five dollars."

"Then you had better give it back to me. Five dollars isn't worth taking."

"You're a cool one, and no mistake," said Jack, surveying our hero with greater respect than he had before manifested. "Do you know that I could wring your neck?"

"Yes, I suppose you could," said Walter, quietly. "You are a great deal stronger than I am."

"Aint you afraid of me?"

"I don't think I am. Why should I be?"

"What's to hinder my killin' you? We're alone in the woods, far from help."

"I don't think you'll do it," said Walter, meeting his gaze steadily.

"You aint a coward, boy; I'll say that for you. Some boys of your age would be scared to death if they was in your place."

"I don't think I am a coward," said Walter, quietly. "Are you going to give me back that pocket-book?"

"Not if I know it; but I'll tell you what you're goin' to do."

"What's that?"

"Hunt up the rest of that money, and pretty quick too."

"What makes you think I have got any more money?"

"Didn't you tell me you sold twenty books, at three dollars and a half? That makes seventy dollars, accordin' to my reckonin'."

"You're right there; but I have sent to Cleveland for some more books, and had to send the money with the order."

This staggered the robber at first, till he remembered what his wife had told him.

"That don't go down," he said roughly. "The old woman saw a big roll of bills when you paid her for your lodgin'. You haven't had any chance of payin' them away."

Walter recalled the covetous glance of the woman when he displayed the bills, and he regretted too late his imprudence in revealing the amount of money he had with him. He saw that it was of no use to attempt to deceive Jack any longer. It might prove dangerous, and could do no good.

"I have some more money," he said; "but I hope you will let me keep it."

"What made you take it out of your pocket-book?"

"Because I thought I should have a visit from you."

"What made you think so?" demanded Jack, rather surprised.

"I can't tell, but I expected a visit, so I took out most of my money and hid it."

"Then you'd better find it again. I can't wait here all night. Is it in your other pocket?"

"No."

"Is that all you can say? Get up, and find me that money, or it'll be the worse for you."

"Then give me the pocket-book and five dollars. I can't get along if you take all my money."

Jack reflected that he could easily take away the pocket-book again, and decided to comply with our hero's request as an inducement for him to find the other money.

"Here it is," he said. "Now get me the rest."

"I hid some money in that closet," said Walter. "I thought you would think of looking there."

No sooner was the closet pointed out than Jack eagerly strode towards it and threw open the door. He entered it, and began to peer about him, holding the candle in his hand.

"Where did you put it?" he inquired, turning to question Walter.

But he had scarcely spoken when our hero closed the

door hastily, and, before Jack could recover from his surprise, had bolted it on the outside. To add to the discomfiture of the imprisoned robber, the wind produced by the violent slamming of the door blew out the candle, and he found himself a captive, in utter darkness.

"Let me out, or I'll murder you!" he roared, kicking the barrier that separated him from his late victim, now his captor.

Walter saw that there was no time to lose. The door, though strong, would probably soon give way before the strength of his prisoner. When the liberation took place, he must be gone. He held the handle of his carpet-bag between his teeth, and, getting out of the window, hung down. The distance was not great, and he alighted upon the ground without injury. Without delay he plunged into the woods, not caring in what direction he went, as long as it carried him away from his dishonest landlord.

CHAPTER XXXI. WALTER'S ESCAPE.

Though Walter was in a room on the second floor, the distance to the ground was not so great but that he could easily hang from the window-sill and jump without injury. Before following him in his flight, we will pause to inquire how the robber, unexpectedly taken captive, fared.

Nothing could have surprised Jack more than this sudden turning of the tables. But a minute since Walter was completely in his power. Now, through the boy's coolness and nerve, his thievish intentions were baffled, and he was placed in the humiliating position of a prisoner in his own house.

"Open the door, or I'll murder you!" he roared, kicking it violently.

There was no reply, for Walter was already half way out of the window, and did not think it best to answer.

Jack kicked again, but the door was a strong one, and, though it shook, did not give way.

"Draw the bolt, I say," roared the captive again, appending an oath, "or I'll wring your neck."

But our hero was already on the ground, and speeding away into the shelter of the friendly woods.

If any man was thoroughly mad, that man was Jack. It was not enough that he had been ingloriously defeated, but the most galling thing about it was that this had been done by a boy.

"I'll make him pay for this!" muttered Jack, furiously.

He saw that Walter had no intention of releasing him, and that his deliverance must come from himself. He kicked furiously, and broke through one of the panels of the door; but still the bolt held, and continued to hold, though he threw himself against the door with all his force.

Meanwhile his wife below had listened intently, at the bottom of the staircase, not without anxiety as to the result. She was a woman, and, though by no means of an amiable disposition, she was not without some humanity. She knew her husband's brutal temper, and she feared that Walter would come to harm. Part of her anxiety was selfish, to be sure, for she dreaded the penalty for her husband; but she was partly actuated by a feeling of rough good-will towards her young guest. She didn't mind his being robbed, for she felt that in some way she had been cheated out of that measure of worldly prosperity which was her due, and she had no particular scruple as to the means of getting even with the world. The fact that Walter, too, had suffered bad fortune increased her good-will towards him, and made her more reluctant that he should be ill-treated.

At first, as she listened, and while the conversation was going on, she heard nothing to excite her alarm. But when her husband had been locked in the closet, and began to kick at the door, there was such a noise that Meg, though misapprehending the state of things, got frightened.

"He's killing the poor boy, I'm afraid," she said, clasping her hands. "Why, why need he be so violent? I told him not to harm him."

Next she heard Jack's voice in angry tones, but could not understand what he said. This was followed by a fresh shower of kicks at the resisting door.

"I would go up if I dared," she thought; "but I am afraid I should see the poor boy dying."

She feared, also, her husband's anger at any interference; for, as she had reason to know, his temper was not of the gentlest. So she stood anxiously at the foot of the staircase, and continued to listen.

Meanwhile Jack, finding he could not release himself readily, bethought himself of his wife.

"Meg!" he called out, in stentorian tones.

His wife heard the summons and made haste to obey it.

She hurried upstairs, and, opening the chamber door,

found herself, to her surprise, in darkness.

"Where are you, Jack?" she asked, in some bewilderment.

"Here," answered her husband.

"Where?" asked Meg; for the tones were muffled by the interposition of the door, and she could not get a clear idea of where her husband was.

"In the closet, you fool! Come and open the door," was the polite reply.

Wondering how her husband could have got into the closet, and, also, what had become of Walter, she advanced hastily to the closet-door, and drew the bolt.

Jack dashed out furiously, cursing in a manner I shall not repeat.

"How came you here, Jack?" asked his wife. "Where's the boy?"

It was so dark that he could not readily discover Walter's flight. He strode to the bedstead, and, kneeling down, began to feel about for him.

"Curse it, the boy's gone!" he exclaimed. "Why didn't you stop him?"

This he said on supposition that Walter had escaped by the stairs.

"I don't know what you mean. I've seen nothing of the boy. Wasn't he here when you came up?"

"Yes, he was, but now he's gone. He must have got out of the window," he added, with a sudden thought.

"I don't understand it," said Meg. "How came you shut up in that closet?"

"The boy sent me in on a fool's errand, and then locked me in."

"Tell me about it, Jack."

Her husband rehearsed the story, heaping execrations upon his own folly for being outwitted by a boy.

"But you've got the pocket-book and the five dollars,"

said his wife, by way of comforting him.

"No, I haven't. I gave them back to him, to get him to tell me where the rest of the money was. I meant to take it away from him again."

"Then he's escaped with all his money?"

"Yes," growled Jack; "he's fooled me completely. But it isn't too late. I may catch him yet. He's hiding in the woods somewhere. If I do get hold of him, I'll give him something to remember me by. I'll learn him to fool me."

"I wouldn't go out to-night, Jack," said his wife. "It's most twelve."

"If I don't go now, I'll lose him. Go downstairs, Meg, and light the candle."

"Did he have the money with him?"

"He said he hid it."

"Then perhaps he left it behind him. He had to go away in a hurry."

"That's so, Meg. Hurry down, and light the candle, and we'll hunt for it."

The suggestion was a reasonable one, and Jack caught at it. If the money were left behind, it would repay him in part for his mortification at having been fooled by a boy, and he might be tempted to let him go. What vexed him most was the idea of having been baffled completely; and the discovery of the money would go far to make things even.

Meg came up with the lighted candle; and they commenced a joint search, first in the closet, where they found the five pennies which Walter had thrown on the floor, and, afterwards, about the room, and particularly the bedding. But the roll of bills was nowhere to be found. Walter had, as we know, carried it away with him. This was the conclusion to which the seekers were ultimately brought.

"The money aint anywhere here," said Jack. "The boy's

got it with him."

"Likely he has," said Meg.

"I'm goin' for him," said her husband. "Go downstairs, Meg, and I'll foller."

"You'd better wait till mornin', Jack," said his wife.

"You're a fool!" he said, unceremoniously. "If I wait till daylight, he'll be out of the woods, and I can't catch him."

"There isn't much chance now. It's dark, and you won't be likely to find him."

"I'll risk that. Anyhow, I'm goin' and so you needn't say any more about it."

Jack descended to the room below, put on his boots and hat, and, opening the outer door, sallied out into the darkness.

He paused before the door in uncertainty.

"I wish I knowed which way he went," he muttered.

There seemed little to determine the choice of direction on the part of the fugitive. There was no regular path, as Jack and his wife were the only dwellers in the forest who had occasion to use one, except such as occasionally strayed in from the outer world. There was, indeed, a path slightly marked, but this Walter could not see in the darkness. Nevertheless, as chance would have it, he struck into it and followed it for some distance.

Having nothing else to determine his course, it was only natural that Jack should take this path. Now that he was already started on his expedition, and found the natural darkness of the night deepened and made more intense by the thick foliage of the forest trees, he realized that his chances of coming upon Walter were by no means encouraging. But he kept on with dogged determination.

"I'd like to catch the young rascal, even if I don't get a penny of the money," he said to himself.

He resolved, in case he was successful, first, to give his victim a severe beating, and next, to convey him home, and keep him for weeks a close prisoner in the very closet in which he had himself been confined. The thought of such an appropriate vengeance yielded him considerable satisfaction, and stimulated him to keep up the search.

CHAPTER XXXII. A STRANGE HIDING-PLACE.

Meanwhile Walter had the advantage of quarter of an hour's start of his pursuer. Jack had indeed been released within five minutes, but he had consumed ten minutes more in searching for the money. It was too dark, however, to make rapid progress. Still Walter pushed on, resolved to put as great a distance as possible between the cabin and himself, for he anticipated pursuit, and judged that, if caught, he would fare badly for the trick he had played upon his host.

He had proceeded perhaps half a mile when he stopped to rest. Two or three times he had tripped over projecting roots which the darkness prevented his seeing in time to avoid.

"I'll rest a few minutes, and then push on," he thought.

It was late, but the excitement of his position prevented him from feeling sleepy. He wished to get out of the woods into some road or open field, where he would be in less danger of encountering Jack, and where perhaps he might find assistance against him.

He was leaning against an immense tree, one of the largest and oldest in the forest. Walter began idly to examine it. He discovered, by feeling, that it was hollow inside. Curiosity led him to examine farther. He ascertained that the interior was eaten out by gradual decay, making a large hollow space inside.

"I shouldn't wonder if I could get in," he said to himself.

He made the attempt, and found that he was correct in his supposition. He could easily stand erect inside.

"That is curious," thought Walter. "The tree must be very old."

He emerged from the trunk, and once more threw himself down beside it. Five minutes later and his attention was drawn by a sound of approaching footsteps. Then came an oath, which sounded startlingly near. It was uttered by Jack, who had tripped over a root, and was picking himself up in no very good humor. The enemy, it appeared, was close upon him.

Walter started to his feet in dismay. His first thought was immediate flight, but if he were heard by Jack, the latter would no doubt be able to run him down.

"What shall I do?" thought Walter, in alarm.

Quickly the hollow trunk occurred to him. He seized his carpet-bag, and with as little delay as possible concealed himself in the interior. He was just in time, for Jack was by this time only a few rods distant. Walter counted upon his passing on; but on reaching the old tree Jack paused, and said aloud, "Where can the young rascal be? I wonder if I have passed him? I'll rest here five minutes. He may straggle along."

With these words he sank upon the ground, in the very same place where Walter had been reclining two minutes before. He was so near that our hero could have put out his hand and touched him.

It was certainly a very uncomfortable situation for Walter. He hardly dared to breathe or to stir lest his enemy should hear him.

"He's led me a pretty tramp," muttered Jack. "I'm as tired as a dog, but I'm bound to get hold of him to-night. If I do, I'll half kill him."

"Then I hope you won't get hold of him," Walter ejaculated inwardly.

He began to wish he had run on instead of seeking this concealment. In the first case, the darkness of the night would have favored him, and even if Jack had heard him it was by no means certain that he would have caught him. Now an unlucky movement or a cough would betray his hiding-place, and there would be no chance of escape. He began to feel his constrained position irksome, but did not dare to seek relief by change of posture.

"I wish he'd go," thought our hero.

But Jack was in no hurry. He appeared to wish to waylay Walter, and was constantly listening to catch the sound of his approach. At last a little relief came. A sound was heard, which Jack suspected might proceed from his late guest. He started to his feet, and walked a few steps away. Walter availed himself of this opportunity to change his position a little.

"It isn't he," said Jack, disappointed. "Perhaps he's gone another way."

He did not throw himself down this time, but remained standing, in evident uncertainty. At length Walter was relieved to hear him say, "Well, I shan't catch him by stopping here, that's sure."

Then he started, and Walter, listening intently, heard the sound of his receding steps. When sufficient time had elapsed, he ventured out from his concealment, and stopped to consider the situation.

What should he do?

It was hardly prudent to go on, for it would only bring him nearer to the enemy. If he ventured back, he would be farther away from the edge of the woods, and might encounter Meg, who might also be in pursuit. He did not feel in danger of capture from this quarter, but the woman might find means of communicating with her husband. On the whole, it seemed safest, for the present at least, to stick to the friendly tree which had proved so good a protector. He stood beside it, watching carefully, intending, whenever peril threatened, to take instant refuge inside. This was not particularly satisfactory, but he hoped Jack would soon tire of the pursuit, and retrace his steps towards the cabin. If he should do that, he would then be safe in continuing his flight.

Jack pushed on, believing that our hero was in advance. It had been a fatiguing day, and this made his present midnight tramp more disagreeable. His hopes of overtaking Walter became fainter and fainter, and nature began to assert her rights. A drowsiness which he found it hard to combat assailed him, and he found he must yield to it for a time at least.

"I wish I was at home, and in bed," he muttered. "I'll lie down and take a short nap, and then start again."

He threw himself down on the ground, and no longer resisted the approaches of sleep. In five minutes his senses were locked in a deep slumber, which, instead of a short nap, continued for several hours.

While he is sleeping we will go back to Walter. He, too, was sleepy, and would gladly have laid down and slept if he had dared. But he felt the peril of his position too sensibly to give way to his feelings. He watched vigilantly for an hour, but nothing could be seen of Jack. That hour seemed to him to creep with snail-like pace.

"I can't stand this watching till morning," he said to himself. "I will find some out-of-the-way place, and try to sleep a little."

Searching about he found such a place as he desired. He lay down, and was soon fast asleep. So pursuer and pursued had yielded to the spell of the same enchantress, and half a mile distant from each other were enjoying welcome repose.

Some hours passed away. The sun rose, and its rays lighted up the dim recesses of the forest. When Walter opened his eyes he could not at first remember where he was. He lifted his head from his carpet-bag which he had used as a pillow, and looked around him in surprise; but recollection quickly came to his aid.

"I must have been sleeping several hours," he said to himself, "for it is now morning. I wonder if the man who was after me has gone home?"

He decided that this was probable, and resolved to make an attempt to reach the edge of the forest. He wanted to get into the region of civilization again, if for no other reason, because he felt hungry, and was likely to remain so as long as he continued in the forest. He now felt fresh and strong, and, taking his carpet-bag in his hand, prepared to start on his journey. But he had scarcely taken a dozen steps when a female figure stepped out from a covert, and he found himself face to face with Meg.

Not knowing but that her husband might be close behind, he started back in alarm and hesitation. She observed this, and said, "You needn't be afraid, boy. I don't want to harm you."

"Is your husband with you?" asked Walter, on his guard.

"No, he isn't. He started out after you before midnight, and hasn't been back since. That made me uneasy, and I came out to look for him."

"I have seen him," said Walter.

"Where and when?" asked the woman, eagerly.

It was strange that such a coarse brute should have inspired any woman with love, but Meg did certainly love her husband, in spite of his frequent bad treatment.

"It must have been within an hour of the time I left your house. He stopped under that tree. That was where I saw him."

"Did he see you?"

"No, I was hidden."

"How long did he stay?"

"Only a few minutes, to get rested, I suppose. Then he went on."

"In what direction?"

"That way."

"I am glad he did not harm you. He was so angry when he started that I was afraid of what would happen if he met you. You must keep out of his way."

"That is what I mean to do if I can," said Walter. "Can you tell me the shortest way out of the woods?"

"Go in that direction," said the woman, pointing, "and half a mile will bring you out."

"It is rather hard to follow a straight path in the woods. If you will act as my guide, I will give you a dollar."

Meg hesitated.

"If my husband should find out that I helped you to escape, he would be very angry."

"Why need he know? You needn't tell him you met me."

The woman hesitated. Finally love of money prevailed.

"I'll do it," she said, abruptly. "Follow me."

She took the lead, and Walter followed closely in her steps. Remembering the night before, he was not wholly assured of her good faith, and resolved to keep his eyes open, and make his escape instantly if he should see any signs of treachery. Possibly Meg might intend to lead him into a trap, and deliver him up to her husband. He was naturally trustful, but his adventures in the cabin taught him a lesson of distrust.

CHAPTER XXXIII. WALTER SHOWS STRATEGY.

Walter followed Meg through the woods. He felt sure that he would not have far to go to reach the open fields. He had been delayed heretofore, not by the distance, but by not knowing in what direction to go.

Few words were spoken between him and Meg. Remembering what had happened at the cabin, and that even now he was fleeing from her husband, he did not feel inclined to be sociable, and her thoughts were divided between the money she was to be paid as the price of her services, and her husband, for whose prolonged absence she could not account.

After walking for fifteen minutes, they came to the edge of the forest. Skirting it was a meadow, wet in parts, for the surface was low.

"Where is the road?" asked Walter.

"You'll have to cross this meadow, and you'll come to it. It isn't mor'n quarter of a mile. You'll find your way well enough without me."

Walter felt relieved at the prospect of a speedy return to the region of civilization. It seemed to him as if he had passed the previous night far away in some wild frontier cabin, instead of in the centre of a populous and thriving neighborhood, within a few miles of several flourishing villages.

He drew out a dollar-bill, and offered it to Meg.

"This is the money I agreed to pay you," he said. "Thank you, besides."

"You haven't much cause to thank me," she said, abruptly. "I would have robbed you if I had the chance."

"I am sorry for that," said Walter. "Money got in that way never does any good."

"Money is sure to do good, no matter how it comes," said the woman, fiercely. "Think of what it will buy!—a comfortable home, ease, luxury, respect. Some time before I die I hope to have as much as I want."

"I hope you will," said Walter; "but I don't think you will find it as powerful as you think."

His words might as well have remained unspoken, for she paid no attention to them. She seemed to be listening intently. Suddenly she clutched his arm.

"I hear my husband's steps," she said, hurriedly. "Fly, or it will be the worse for you."

"Thank you for the caution," said Walter, roused to the necessity of immediate action.

"Don't stop to thank me. Go!" she said, stamping her foot impatiently.

He obeyed at once, and started on a run across the meadow.

A minute later, Jack came in sight.

"What, Meg, are you here?" he said, in surprise.

"Yes; I got anxious about you, because you did not come home. I was afraid something had happened to you."

"What could happen to me?" he retorted, contemptuously. "I'm not a baby. Have you seen the boy?"

He did not wait for an answer, for, looking across the meadow, he saw the flying figure of our hero.

"There he is, now!" he exclaimed, in a tone of fierce satisfaction.

"Let him go, Jack!" pleaded Meg, who, in spite of herself, felt a sympathy for the boy who, like herself, had been unfortunate.

He threw off the hand which she had placed upon his arm, saying, contemptuously, "You're a fool!" and then dashed off in pursuit of Walter.

Walter had the start, and had already succeeded in placing two hundred yards between himself and his pursuer. But Jack was strong and athletic, and could run faster than a boy of fifteen, and the distance between the two constantly diminished. Walter looked over his shoulder, as he ran, and, brave as he was, there came over him a sickening sensation of fear as he met the fierce, triumphant glance of his enemy.

"Stop!" called out Jack, hoarsely.

Walter did not answer, neither did he obey. He was determined to hold out to the last, and when he surrendered it would be only as a measure of necessity.

"Are you going to stop or not? You'd better," growled Jack.

Walter still remained silent; but his heart bounded with sudden hope as he saw before him a means of possible escape. Only a few rods in advance was a deep ditch, at least twelve feet wide, over which a single plank was thrown as a bridge for foot-passengers. Walter summoned his energies, and sped like a deer forward and over the bridge, when, stooping down, he hastily pulled it over after him, thus cutting off his enemy's advance. Jack saw his intention, and tried to reach the edge of the ditch soon enough to prevent it. But he was just too late.

Baffled and enraged, he looked across the gulf which separated him from his intended victim.

"Put back that plank," he roared, with an oath.

"I would rather not," said Walter, who stood facing him on the other side, hot and excited.

"I'll kill you if I get at you," said Jack, shaking his fist menacingly.

"What have I done to you?" asked Walter, quietly. "Why do you want to harm me?"

"Didn't you lock me up in the closet last night?"

"You wanted to take my money."

"I'll have it yet."

"It was all I could do," said Walter, who did not wish to excite any additional anger in his already irritated foe. "I haven't got but a little money, and I wanted to keep it."

"Money isn't the only thing you may lose," said the ruffian, significantly. "Put back that plank. Do you hear me?"

"Yes," said Walter; "I hear, but I cannot do it."

"You're playin' a dangerous game, young one," said Jack. "Perhaps you think I can't get over."

"I don't think you can," said Walter, glancing at the width of the ditch.

"You may find yourself mistaken."

Walter did not answer.

"Will you put back that plank?" demanded Jack, once more.

"No," answered Walter.

"You'll be sorry for it then, you young cub!" said Jack, fiercely.

He walked back about fifty feet, and then faced round. His intention was clear enough. He meant to jump over the ditch. Could he do it? That was the question which suggested itself to the anxious consideration of our hero. If the ground had been firm on the other side, such a jump for a grown man would not have been by any means a remarkable one. But the soft, spongy soil was unfavorable for a spring. Still it was possible that Jack might succeed. If he did, was there any help for Walter?

Our hero took the plank, and put it over his shoulder, moving with it farther down the edge. An idea had occurred to him, which had not yet suggested itself to Jack, or the latter might have been less confident of success.

Jack stood still for a moment, and then, gathering up his strength, dashed forward. Arrived at the brink, he made a spring, but the soft bank yielded him no support. He fell short of the opposite bank by at least two feet, and, to his anger and disgust, landed in the water and slime at the bottom of the ditch. With a volley of execrations, he scrambled out, landing at last, but with the loss of one boot, which had been drawn off by the clinging mud in which it had become firmly planted. Still he was on the same side with Walter, and the latter was now in his power. This was what he thought; but an instant later he saw his mistake. Walter had stretched the plank over the ditch a few rods further up, and was passing over it in safety.

Jack ran hastily to the spot, hoping to gain possession of the plank which had been of such service to his opponent, and want of which had entailed such misfortunes upon him. But Walter was too quick for him. The plank was drawn over, and again he faced his intended victim with the width of the ditch between.

He looked across at Walter with a glance of baffled rage. It was something new to him to be worsted by a boy, and it mortified him and angered him to such an extent that, had he got hold of him at that moment, murder might have been committed.

"Put down that plank, and come across," he called out.

Walter did not reply.

"Why don't you answer, you rascal?"

"You know well enough what I would say," said Walter. "I don't care to come."

"I shall get hold of you sooner or later."

"Perhaps you will," said Walter; "but not if I can help it."

"You're on the wrong side of the ditch. You can't escape."

"So are you on the wrong side. You can't get home without crossing."

"I can keep you there all day."

"I can stand it as well as you," said Walter.

He felt bolder than at first, for he appreciated the advantage which he had in possessing the plank. True the situation was not a comfortable one, and he would have gladly exchanged it for one that offered greater security. Still, on the whole, he felt cool and calm, and waited patiently for the issue.

CHAPTER XXXIV. DELIVERANCE.

Jack might have waded back again across the ditch without inflicting much additional damage upon his already wet and miry clothing; but he fancied that Walter was in his power, and hoped he would capitulate. To this end, he saw that it was necessary to reassure him, and deceive him as to his own intentions.

"Come across, boy," he said, softening his tone. "You needn't be afraid. I didn't mean nothing. I was only tryin' to see if I couldn't frighten you a little."

"I'm very well off where I am," said Walter. "I think I'll stay where I am."

"You won't want to stay there all day."

"I'd rather stay here all day than be on the same side with you."

"You needn't be afraid."

"I am not afraid," said Walter.

"You think I want to hurt you."

"I think I am safer on this side."

"Come, boy, I'll make a bargain with you. You've put me to a good deal of trouble."

"I don't see that."

"You locked me up in the closet, and you've kept me all night huntin' after you."

"You were not obliged to hunt after me, and as for locking you up in the closet, it was the only way I had of saving my money."

Jack did not care to answer Walter's argument, but proceeded: "Now I've got you sure, but I'll do the fair thing. If you'll come across and pay me ten dollars for my trouble, I'll let you go without hurtin' you."

"What's to prevent you taking all my money, if you get me over there?"

"Haven't I said I wouldn't?"

"You might forget your promise," said Walter, whose confidence in Jack's word was by no means great. A man who would steal probably would not be troubled by many scruples on the subject of violating his word.

"If you don't come, I'll take every cent, and give you a beating beside," said Jack, his anger gaining the ascendency.

"Well, what are you goin' to do about it?" demanded Jack, after a brief pause.

"I'll stay where I am."

"I can come over any time, and get hold of you."

"Perhaps you can," said Walter. "I'll take the risk."

"I'll wait a while," thought Jack. "He'll come round after a while."

He sat down, and taking a clay pipe from his pocket, filled the bowl with tobacco, and commenced smoking. Walter perceived that he was besieged, but kept cool, and clung to his plank, which was his only hope of safety. He began to speculate as to the length of time the besieging force would hold out. He was already hungry, and there was a prospect of his being starved into a surrender, or there would have been, if luckily his opponent had not been also destitute of provisions. In fact, the besieging party soon became disorganized from this cause. A night in the open air had given keenness to Jack's appetite, and he felt an uncomfortable craving for food.

"I wish Meg would come along," he muttered. "I feel empty."

But Meg did not come. She stood for a few minutes in the edge of the woods, and watched her husband's pursuit of Walter. She saw his failure to overtake his intended victim, and this made her easier in her mind. I do not wish to represent her as better than she was. Her anxiety was chiefly for her husband. She did not wish him to commit any act of violence which would put him without the pale of the law. It was this consideration, rather than a regard for Walter's safety, that influenced her, though she felt some slight interest in our hero. She went home, feeling that she could do no good in staying. Jack resented her disappearance.

"She might know I wanted some breakfast," he growled to himself. "As long as she gets enough to eat herself, she cares little for me."

This censure was not deserved. Meg was not a good woman, but she was devoted to the coarse brute whom she called husband, and was at any time ready to sacrifice her own comfort to his.

Two hours passed, and still besieger and besieged eyed each other from opposite sides of the bank. Jack grew more and more irritable as the cravings of his appetite increased, and the slight hope that Meg might appear with some breakfast was dissipated. Walter also became more hungry, but showed no signs of impatience.

At this time a boy was seen coming across the meadow. Jack espied him, and the idea struck him that he might through him lay in a stock of provisions.

"Come here, boy," he said. "Where do you live?"

The boy pointed to a small farm-house half a mile distant.

"Do you want to earn some money?"

"I dunno," said the boy, who had no objections to the money, but, knowing Jack's shady reputation, was in doubt as to what was expected of him.

"Go home, and get a loaf of bread and some cold meat, and bring me, and I'll give you half a dollar."

"Didn't you bring your luncheon?" asked the boy.

"No, I came away without it, and I can't spare time to go back."

It occurred to the boy, noticing Jack's lazy posture, that business did not appear to be very driving with the man whose time was so valuable.

"Perhaps mother won't give me the bread and meat," he said.

"You can give her half the money."

The boy looked across to Walter, wondering what kept him on the other side. Our hero saw a chance of obtaining help.

"I'll give you a dollar," he called out, "if you'll go and tell somebody that this man is trying to rob me of all my money. I slept in his house last night, and he tried to rob me there. Now he will do the same if he can get hold of me."

"If you tell that, I'll wring your neck," exclaimed Jack. "It's all a lie. The boy slept at my house, as he says, and stole some money from me. He escaped, but I'm bound to get it back if I stay here all day."

"That is not true," said Walter. "Carry my message, and I will give you a dollar, and will, besides, reward the men that come to my assistance." The boy looked from one to the other in doubt what to do.

"If you want your head broke, you'll do as he says," said Jack, rather uneasy. "He won't pay what he promises."

"You shall certainly be paid," said Walter.

"You'd better shut up, or it'll be the worse for you," growled Jack. "Go and get my breakfast quick, boy, and I'll pay you the fifty cents."

"All right," said the boy, "I'll go."

He turned, but when he was behind Jack, so that the latter could not observe him, he made a sign to Walter that he would do as he wished.

Fifteen minutes later Jack rose to his feet. An idea had occurred to him. At the distance of a furlong there was a rail-fence. It occurred to him that one of these rails would enable him to cross the ditch, and get at his victim. He was not afraid Walter would escape, since he could easily turn back and capture him if he ventured across.

Walter did not understand his design in leaving the ditch.

Was it possible that he meant to raise the siege? This seemed hardly probable. He watched, with some anxiety, the movements of his foe, fearing some surprise.

When Jack reached the fence, and began to pull out one of the rails he understood his object. His position was evidently becoming more dangerous.

Jack came back with a triumphant smile upon his face.

"Now, you young cub," he said, "I've got you!"

Walter watched him warily, and lowered the plank, ready to convert it into a bridge as soon as necessary. Jack put down the rail. It was long enough to span the ditch, but was rather narrow, so that some caution was needful in crossing it. Walter had moved several rods farther up, and thrown the plank across. Though his chances of escape from the peril that menaced him seemed to have diminished since his enemy was also provided with a bridge and it became now a question of superior speed, Walter was not alarmed. Indeed his prospects of deliverance appeared brighter than ever, for he caught sight of two men approaching across the meadow, and he suspected that they were sent by the boy whom he had hired. These men had not yet attracted the attention of Jack, whose back was turned towards them. He crossed the rail, and, at the same time, Walter crossed the plank. This he threw across, and then, leaving it on the bank, set out on a quick run.

"Now I'll catch him," thought Jack, with exultation; but he quickly caught sight of our hero's reinforcements. He saw that his game was up, and he abandoned it. His reputation was too well known in the neighborhood for the story he had told to the boy to gain credence. He was forced to content himself with shaking his fist at Walter, and then, in discomfiture, returned to the woods, where he made up for his disappointment by venting his spite on Meg. She would have fared worse, had he known that Walter had found his way out of the wood through her guidance.

CHAPTER XXXV. THE LAST OF JACK MANGUM.

"What's the matter?" asked one of the two men as Walter came up.

"I got lost in the woods, and passed the night in that man's house," said our hero. "He tried to rob me, but I locked him in the closet, and jumped out of the window and escaped. This morning he got on my track, and would have caught me but for the ditch."

"You locked him in the closet!" repeated the other. "How were you able to do that? You are only a boy, while he is a strong man."

Walter explained the matter briefly.

"That was pretty smart," said Peter Halcomb, for this was the name of the man who questioned him. "You're able to take care of yourself."

"I don't know how it would turn out, if you hadn't come up."

"I happened to be at home when my boy came and told me that Jack Mangum had offered him fifty cents for some breakfast. He told me about you also, and, as I suspected Jack was up to some of his tricks, I came along."

"I am very much obliged to you," said Walter, "and I hope you'll let me pay you for your trouble."

"I don't want any pay, but you may pay my boy what you promised him, if you want to."

"I certainly will; and I never paid away money with more pleasure. As I haven't had anything to eat since yesterday afternoon, I should like to have you direct me to the nearest place where I can get some breakfast."

"Come to my house; I guess my wife can scare up some breakfast for you. She'll be glad to see the boy that got the better of Jack Mangum."

"How long has this Jack Mangum lived about here?"

asked Walter, after accepting with thanks the offer of a breakfast.

"About five years. He's been in the county jail twice during that time, and there's a warrant out for him now. He's a confirmed thief. He'd rather steal any time than earn an honest living."

"Has he ever stolen anything from you?"

"I've missed some of my chickens from time to time, and, though I didn't catch him taking them, I've no doubt he was the thief. Once I lost a lamb, and I suppose it went in the same direction."

"So there is a warrant out for him now?"

"Yes, and I expect he'll be taken in a day or two. In that case he'll have the privilege of a few months' free board in the county jail."

"Where is the jail?"

"In T——."

"That's the town I'm going to."

"Is it? Do your folks live there?"

"No, I'm travelling on business."

"What's your business?" asked the farmer.

The question was an abrupt one, but was not meant to be rude. In country towns everybody feels that he has a right to become acquainted with the business of any one with whom he comes in contact, even in its minutest details. Walter understood this, having himself lived in a country village, and answered without taking offence:—

"I am a book-agent."

"Be you? How do you make it pay?"

"Pretty well, but I can tell better by and by; I've only been in it a week."

"You're pretty young to be a book-peddler Where do your folks live?"

"In New York."

"You've come some ways from home."

"Yes; I thought I should like to see the country."

"How old are you?"

"Fifteen."

"You'll make a smart man if you keep on."

"I hope I shall," said Walter, modestly; "but I am afraid you overrate me."

"I'll tell you what I judge from. A boy of fifteen that can get the better of Jack Mangum is smart, and no mistake."

"I hope I shall realize your prediction," returned Walter, who naturally felt pleased with the compliment. Like most boys, he liked to be considered smart, although he did not allow himself to be puffed up by inordinate ideas of his own importance, as is the case with many of his age.

While this conversation was going on, they had been walking towards the farm-house in which Peter Holcomb lived. It was an humble one-story building, with an attic above. On each side of it were broad fields, some under cultivation; and there was an appearance of thrift and comfort despite the smallness of the house.

"Come in," said Peter, leading the way. "John," he added, addressing the hired man, who had accompanied him, "you may go into the potato field and hoe. I'll be out directly."

Walter followed him into a broad, low room,—the kitchen,—in which Mrs. Holcomb, a pleasant looking woman, was engaged in cooking.

"Mary," said her husband, "can't you scare up some breakfast for this young man? He stopped at Jack Mangum's last night, and didn't like his accommodations well enough to stay to breakfast."

"You don't say so," repeated Mrs. Holcomb her countenance expressing curiosity. "That's about the last place I'd want to stop at."

"I shouldn't want to go there again," said Walter; "but I

didn't know anything about the man, or I would rather have stayed out in the woods."

"Well, Mary, how about the breakfast?"

"I guess I can find some," said she. "Sit right down here, and I'll see what I can do for you."

She went to the pantry, and speedily reappeared with some cold meat, a loaf of bread, and some fresh butter, which she placed on the table.

"I've got some hot water," she said, "and, in about five minutes, I can give you some warm tea. It won't be much of a breakfast, but if you'll stop for dinner, I can give you something better."

"It looks nice," said Walter, "and I don't know when I have been so hungry."

At this moment the farmer's boy, who had served as Walter's messenger, came into the kitchen.

"You got away," he said, smiling.

"Yes, thanks to you," said Walter. "Here is what I promised you."

"I don't know as I ought to take it," said the boy, hesitating, though he evidently wanted it.

"You will do me a favor by accepting it," said Walter. "You got me out of a bad scrape. Besides, you had a chance to earn some money from Jack Mangum."

"I wouldn't have done anything for him, at any rate. He's a thief."

Finally Peter, for he was named after his father, accepted the dollar, and, sitting down by Walter, asked him about his adventure in the wood, listening with great interest to the details.

"I wouldn't have dared to do as you did," he said.

"Perhaps you would if you had been obliged to."

By this time the tea was steeped, and Walter's breakfast was before him. He made so vigorous an onslaught upon the bread and meat that he was almost ashamed of his appetite; but

Mrs. Holcomb evidently felt flattered at the compliment paid to her cookery, and watched the demolition of the provisions with satisfaction.

"You had better stop to dinner," she said. "We shall have some roast meat and apple-pudding."

"Thank you," said Walter; "but I have eaten enough to last me for several hours. Can you tell me how far it is to the next town?"

"About five miles. I'm going to ride over there in about an hour. If you'll wait till then I'll take you over."

Walter very readily consented to wait. He was rather afraid that if he ventured to walk he might find Jack Mangum waiting to waylay him somewhere in the road, and he had no desire for a second encounter with him.

The farmer absolutely refused to accept pay for breakfast, though Walter urged it. It was contrary to his ideas of hospitality.

"We don't keep a tavern," he said; "and we never shall miss the little you ate. Come again and see us if you come back this way."

"Thank you," said Walter, "I will accept your invitation with pleasure, but I shall not feel like calling on Mr. Mangum."

"I've no doubt he would be glad to see you," said Peter Holcomb, smiling.

"Yes, he was very sorry to have me leave him last night."

Walter thought he had seen the last of Jack Mangum; but he was mistaken. Three days later, while walking in the main street of T——, with a book under his arm, for he had received a fresh supply from the agent at Cleveland, he heard the sound of wheels. Looking up, he saw a wagon approaching, containing two men. One of them, as he afterwards learned, was the sheriff. The other he immediately recognized as Jack Mangum. There was no mistaking his sinister face and forbidding scowl. He had been taken early that morning by the sheriff, who, with a couple of men to assist him, had visited the cabin in the forest, and, despite the resistance offered by Jack, who was aided by his wife, he had been bound, and was now being conveyed to jail. He also looked up and recognized Walter. His face became even more sinister, as he shook his fist at our hero.

"I'll be even with you some day, you young cub!" he exclaimed.

"Not if I can help it," thought Walter; but he did not answer in words.

He was rather gratified to hear the next day that Jack had been sentenced to six months' imprisonment. He felt some pity, however, for Meg, who might have been a good woman if she had been married to a different man.

CHAPTER XXXVI. JOSHUA BIDS GOOD-BY TO STAPLETON.

Leaving Walter busily engaged in selling books, we will glance at the Drummond household, and inquire how the members of that interesting family fared after Walter's departure.

Joshua's discontent increased daily. He was now eighteen, and his father absolutely refused to increase his allowance of twenty-five cents a week, which was certainly ridiculously small for a boy of his age.

"If you want money you must work for it," he said.

"How much will you give me if I will go into your store?" asked Joshua.

"Fifty cents a week and your board."

"I get my board now."

"You don't earn it."

"I don't see why I need to," said Joshua. "Aint you a rich man?"

"No, I'm not," said his father; "and if I were I am not going to waste my hard-earned money on supporting you extravagantly."

"There's no danger of that," sneered Joshua, "We live meaner than any family in town."

"You needn't find fault with your victuals, as long as you get them free," retorted his father.

"If you'll give me two dollars a week, I'll come into the store."

"Two dollars!" exclaimed Mr. Drummond. "Are you crazy?"

"You think as much of a cent as most people do of a dollar," said Joshua, bitterly. "Two dollars isn't much for the son of a rich man."

"I have already told you that I am not rich."

"You can't help being rich," said Joshua, "for you don't

spend any money."

"I've heard enough of your impudence," said his father, angrily. "If you can get more wages than I offer you, you are at liberty to engage anywhere else."

"Tom Burton gets a dollar and a quarter a day for pegging shoes," said Joshua. "He dresses twice as well as I do."

"He has to pay his board out of it."

"He only pays three dollars a week, and that leaves him four dollars and a half clear."

"So you consider Tom Burton better off than you are?"

"Yes."

"Then I'll make you an offer. I'll get you a place in a shoe-shop, and let you have all you earn over and above three dollars a week, which you can pay for your board."

Joshua seemed by no means pleased with this proposal.

"I'm not going to work in a shoe-shop," he said, sullenly.

"Why not?"

"It's a dirty business."

"Yet you were envying Tom Burton just now."

"It'll do well enough for him. He's a poor man's son."

"So was I a poor man's son. I had to work when I was a boy, and that's the way I earned all I have. Not that I am rich," added Mr. Drummond, cautiously, for he was afraid the knowledge of his wealth would tempt his family to expect a more lavish expenditure, and this would not by any means suit him.

"You didn't work in a shoe-shop."

"I should have been glad of the chance to do it, for I could have earned more money that way than by being errand-boy in a store. It's just as honorable to work in a shop as to be clerk in a store."

Though we are not partial to Mr. Drummond, he was undoubtedly correct in this opinion, and it would be well if boys would get over their prejudice against trades, which, on the whole, offer more assured prospects of ultimate prosperity than the crowded city and country stores.

This conversation was not particularly satisfactory to Joshua. As he now received his board and twenty-five cents a week, he did not care to enter his father's store for only twenty-five cents a week more. Probably it would have been wiser for Mr. Drummond to grant his request, and pay him two dollars a week. With this inducement Joshua might have formed habits of industry. He would, at all events, have been kept out of mischief, and it would have done him good to earn his living by hard work. Mr. Drummond's policy of mortifying his pride by doling out a weekly pittance so small that it kept him in a state of perpetual discontent was far from wise. Most boys appreciate considerable liberality, and naturally expect to be treated better as they grow older. Joshua, now nearly nineteen, found himself treated like a boy of twelve, and he resented it. It set him speculating about his father's death, which would leave him master, as he hoped, of the "old man's" savings. It is unfortunate when such a state of feeling comes to exist between a father and a son. The time came, and that speedily, when Mr. Drummond bitterly repented that he had not made some concessions to Joshua.

Finding his father obstinate, Joshua took refuge at first in sullenness, and for several days sat at the table without speaking a word to his father, excepting when absolutely obliged to do so. Mr. Drummond, however, was not a sensitive man, and troubled himself very little about Joshua's moods.

"He'll get over it after a while," he said to himself. "If he'd rather hold his tongue, I don't care."

Next Joshua began to consider whether there was any way in which to help himself.

"If I only had a hundred dollars," he thought, "I'd go to New York, and see if I couldn't get a place in a store."

That, he reflected, would be much better and more agreeable than being in a country store. He would be his own master, and would be able to put on airs of importance whenever he came home on a vacation. But his father would give him no help in securing such a position, and he could not go to the city without money. As for a hundred dollars, it might as well be a million, so far as he had any chance of securing it.

While he was thinking this matter over, a dangerous thought entered his mind. His father, he knew, had a small brass-nailed trunk, in which he kept his money and securities. He had seen him going to it more than once.

"I wonder how much he's got in it?" thought Joshua. "As it's all coming to me some day there's no harm in my knowing."

There seemed little chance of finding out, however. The trunk was always locked, and Mr. Drummond carried the key about with him in his pocket. If he had been a careless man, there might have been some chance of his some day leaving the trunk unlocked, or mislaying the key; but in money matters Mr. Drummond was never careless. Joshua would have been obliged to wait years, if he had depended upon this contingency.

One day, however, Joshua found in the road a bunch of keys of various sizes attached to a ring. He cared very little to whom they belonged, but it flashed upon him at once that one of these keys might fit his father's strong-box. He hurried home at once with his treasure, and ran upstairs breathless with excitement.

He knew where the trunk was kept. Mr. Drummond, relying on the security of the lock, kept it in the closet of his bed-chamber.

"Where are you going, Joshua?" asked his mother.
"Upstairs, to change my clothes," was the answer.
"I've got a piece of pie for you."

"I'll come down in five minutes."

Joshua made his way at once to the closet, and, entering, began to try his keys, one after the other. The very last one was successful in opening the trunk.

Joshua trembled with excitement as he saw the contents of the trunk laid open to his gaze. He turned over the papers nervously, hoping to come upon some rolls of bills. In one corner he found fifty dollars in gold pieces. Besides these, there were some mortgages, in which he felt little interest. But among the contents of the trunk were some folded papers which he recognized at once as United States Bonds. Opening one of them, he found it to be a Five-Twenty Bond for five hundred dollars.

Five hundred dollars! What could he not do with five hundred dollars! He could go to the city, and board, enjoying himself meanwhile, till he could find a place. His galling dependence would be over, and he would be his own master. True it would be a theft, but Joshua had an excuse ready.

"It will all be mine some day," he said to himself. "It's only taking a part of my own in advance."

He seized the gold and the bond, and, hastily concealing both in his breast-pocket, went downstairs, first locking the trunk, and putting it away where he found it.

"What's the matter, Joshua?" asked his mother, struck by his nervous and excited manner.

"Nothing," he answered, shortly.

"Are you well?"

"I've got a little headache,—that is all."

"Perhaps you'd better not eat anything then."

"It won't do me any harm. I'll take a cup of tea, if you've got any."

"I can make some in five minutes."

Joshua ate his lunch, and, going upstairs again, came down speedily, arrayed in his best clothes. He got out of the house without his mother seeing him, and made his way to a railway station four miles distant, where he purchased a ticket for New York.

He took a seat by a window, and, as the car began to move, he said to himself, in exultation,

"Now I am going to see life."

CHAPTER XXXVII. CONCLUSION.

Three months later Walter arrived at Columbus, the capital of the State, after a business tour of considerable length, during which he had visited from twenty to thirty different towns and villages. He had now got used to the business, and understood better what arguments to employ with those whom he wished to purchase his book. The consequence was, that he had met with a degree of success which exceeded his anticipations. He had tested his powers, and found that they were adequate to the task he had undertaken,—that of earning his own living. He had paddled his own canoe thus far without assistance, and he felt confident that, if his health continued good, he should be able to do so hereafter.

After eating supper, and spending an hour or two in the public room of the hotel, Walter went up to his room. Here he took out a blank-book, in which he kept an account of his sales and expenditures, and, taking a piece of paper, figured up the grand result. He wished to know just how he stood.

After a brief computation, he said, with satisfaction, "I have sold two hundred and eighty books, which gives a gross profit of three hundred and fifty dollars. My expenses have been exactly two hundred and sixty-three dollars. That leaves me eighty-seven dollars net profit."

This was a result which might well yield Walter satisfaction. He was only fifteen, and this was his first business experience. Moreover, he was nearly a thousand miles away from home and friends, surrounded by strangers. Yet, by his energy and business ability, he had been able to pay all his expenses, and these, of course, were considerable, as he was constantly moving, and yet had made a dollar a day clear profit.

"That is rather better than working for my board in Mr. Drummond's store," he reflected. "I am afraid it would have taken me a long time to make my fortune if I had stayed there. I wonder how my amiable cousin Joshua is getting along."

This thought led to the sudden recollection that he had written to Mr. Shaw, asking him to write to the hotel at Columbus where he was now stopping, giving him any news that he might consider interesting. Such a letter might be awaiting him.

He went downstairs, and approached the clerk.

"Have any letters been received here for me?" he inquired.

"What name?" asked the clerk.

"Walter Conrad."

"There is a letter for that address. It was received a week since."

"Give it to me," said Walter, eagerly.

He took the letter, and recognized at once in the address Clement Shaw's irregular handwriting. Cut off, as he had been for over a month, from all communication with former friends, he grasped the letter with a sensation of joy, and hurried back to his room to read it quietly, and without risk of interruption.

The letter ran as follows:—

"My dear young Friend: I have just received your letter asking me to write you at Columbus. I am glad to obtain your address, as I have a matter of importance to speak of. First, however, let me congratulate you on the success you have met with as a book-agent. It is not a business to which I should advise you to devote yourself permanently; but I have no doubt that the experience which you acquire, and the necessary contact into which it brings you with different classes of people, will do you good, while the new scenes which it brings before your eyes will gratify the natural love of adventure which you share in common with those of your age. When you set out, I had misgivings as to your success, I admit. It was certainly an arduous undertaking for a boy of fifteen; but you have already demonstrated that you are able to *paddle your own canoe*; and I shall hereafter feel confident of your success in life, so far at least as relates to earning your living. That you may also be successful in building up a good character, and taking an honorable position among your fellow-men, I earnestly hope.

"I now come to the business upon which I wish to speak to you.

"You will remember that a man named James Wall was prominently identified with the Great Metropolitan Mining Company, by which your poor father lost his fortune. Indeed, this Wall, who is a plausible sort of fellow, was the one who induced him to embark in this disastrous speculation. I suspect he has feathered his own nest pretty well already, and that he intends to do so still more. I was surprised to hear from him some ten days since. I will not copy the letter, but send you the substance of it. He reports that in winding up the affairs of the company, there is a prospect of realizing two per cent. for the stockholders, which, as your father owned a thousand shares, would yield two thousand dollars. It may be some time, he adds, before the dividend will be declared and paid. He professes a willingness, however, to pay two thousand dollars cash for a transfer of your father's claims upon the company.

"Now, two thousand dollars are not to be despised; but, my impression is, that such a man as James Wall would never have made such an offer if he had not expected the assets would amount to considerable more than two per cent. I am unwilling to close with the offer until I know more about the affairs of the company. Here it has struck me that you can be of assistance. This Wall lives in a town named Portville, in Wisconsin, on the shore of Lake Superior. I would suggest that you change your name, go at once to Portville, and find out what you can. I can give you no instructions, but must trust to your own native shrewdness, in which I feel sure you are not deficient. If it should be necessary to give up your present business, do so without hesitation, since the other business is of more importance. I expect you to start at once; and I will write Mr. Wall that I have his offer under consideration. If you need money, draw upon me.

"I hear that Joshua Drummond has run away from home, carrying away considerable money belonging to his father. The latter appears to lament the loss of his money more than of his son.

"I remain your sincere friend,
"Clement Shaw."

This letter gave Walter considerable food for reflection. He determined to wind up his book agency, and leave as soon as possible for Portville. It was encouraging to think that, in any event, he was likely to realize two thousand dollars from the mining shares, which he had looked upon as valueless. Besides, he felt there was good reason to hope they would prove even more valuable.

Three days later, having closed his accounts as agent, he started for Portville. Those of my readers who may desire to follow him in his new experiences, and learn his success, as well as those who feel desirous of ascertaining Joshua Drummond's fortunes, are referred to the next volume of this series, to be called